Enchanted by the Light

15 Short Stories

Celebrating

Christmas in New Mexico

by

Hank Bruce

Enchanted by the Light

15 Short Stories
Celebrating
Christmas in New Mexico
by
Hank Bruce

Published by Petals & Pages Press © 2011

Petals & Pages Press
860 Polaris Blvd SE
Rio Rancho, NM   87124
petals_pages@msn.com   http://petalsandpagespress.weebly.com

Acknowledgments

A special thanks to the people who inspired these stories. While these are fictional observations of this most enchanting season of the year, each was inspired by real people going about the business of living life on their own terms, in their own way; some surviving, others thriving. All are beacons of light on a dark winter's night, each an enchanting ray of hope for all humanity. Thanks to my wife Tomi Jill Folk for her support, advice, editing and encouragement. Thanks to Jon Folk and Nancy Boyer for reading these stories and providing encouragement. A special thanks to Kevin and Miguel, two great representatives of the people who work in the US Postal Service. Their combination of professionalism and humanity made the last story, a true story, possible.

These stories were written as gifts for family and friends over the past decade. Many were created for our grandchildren, Alex, Ethan and Julia, each enchanting in their own way. Others were shared with friends old and new. If you enjoy these stories or are touched by them, please share them with your family and friends. Perhaps someone will smile, think good thoughts about all humanity, relax and enjoy the season, and the enchantment of it all.

Cover design and photos by Tomi Jill Folk

Welcome to
Christmas in New Mexico

This collection of short stories celebrates the diversity of New Mexico's people, cultures and landscapes. Christmas isn't just a marketplace holiday, nor is it a narrow observance of tradition, or the remembrance of an event dimmed by the distance of a couple thousand years.

This is the one time of the year when we can set free the light that shines within each and every one of us. For a few days, or weeks, we allow ourselves the opportunity to glow with peace and good will. The light within vanquishes the fear and anger for just a moment in time, but within that moment is the hope of all humanity.

For each of these stories, this fifth season of the year is a special time, with spirituality that transcends the church pew. This is the season we experience with the senses. After all, New Mexico is a place where "red and green" doesn't refer to decorations, but rather the dinner table choice of red or green chile. During this most intense time of the year, we experience with more than the physical senses. We have the opportunity to experience our sense of belonging, sense of place, sense of hope, sense of peace, and most definitely, our sense of humor.

Our journey through life is a matter of discovery, sharing, caring for one another, and being the gift, more than receiving the gift. Christmas may be the moment in time when we shine, but each of us is a gift every day of our lives, and so is everyone we chance to meet on this journey for which there is no road map. But we do have each other, friend or stranger, to light the way. Hope you are enchanted by the light, and that you are the light for others during this season and every tomorrow. Hopefully, you will enjoy these stories and make friends with each of these characters. Some flawed, others scarred, but all are delightfully human.

Peace, Hank

Table of Contents

Enchanted by the Light

New Mexico seems to attract more than its fair share of creative people; photographers and poets, artists and writers, singers and dancers, jewelers and gardeners. It has been said that the big sky with its abundant bright desert sun is what inspires these minds. Others say it's the perspective from the mountains, where the air is thinner and the spirit closer to the power of the sun that we find so enchanting.

It has also been said that these creative souls are a gift to the universe. While we agree that these people are great gifts, they are not alone in their ability to share the light, or be the light. We are all enchanted by the lights of New Mexico, both the natural light and the light we capture, color, design, and display, including the light within each of us.

The following is a Christmas story about light, and those of us who are too often overlooked, whose gifts are not fully appreciated. Enjoy, and perhaps, let yourself be enchanted by the light, too.

Mac celebrated his ninetieth birthday this week, twelve days before Christmas. For years he has been our Kokopelli figure, wandering the neighborhood with the black garbage bag slung over his shoulder, collecting the aluminum cans the careless have discarded. Some look down on Mac, call him a scavenger, or a crazy old man. Children tease and taunt, but this old man is neither crazy nor ignorant. His reality is both bitter and sweet. Mac is a hero, a wounded veteran of the Second World War. But he is also a wounded veteran of life, who, like all of us, is gradually losing that battle.

He lives in the light and shadow of the long ago yesterdays, while today lies shattered within his mind. Images from childhood, and distant memories from long ago remain crisp and clear. These are the mental treasures that flash through his mind in brilliant technicolor. It is the past still warm that's hazy, disconnected, like attempting to put together the pieces of a jigsaw puzzle without the picture on the box to guide you.

Mac can list for you all the aches and pains that savage his aging body, but he continues to walk the streets, collecting his cans. Great bags full of cans fill his garage, waiting for a neighbor with an afternoon free to take him and his accumulation of aluminum, copper wire and other metal scraps harvested from construction sites and neighborhood garbage cans to the recycling center. There he will trade the fruits of his labor for the cash needed to help pay for the list of medications that keep his aging body functioning. This pocket full of dollars he receives also goes toward the few lottery tickets he purchases every week, living in eternal hope of being a winner.

He almost daily knocks on our door, seeking a ride to the Wal-Mart or simply to his home up the hill a few blocks. It's a ritual now. He comes into the living room, greeted by our dogs who lead him to the recliner. While the dogs serve as friendly hosts, we heat a mug of apple juice for him. He tells the same stories over and over again, because he can't remember telling them to us before. We hear about being left for dead on the battlefield in France, about General Patton running out of medals before that officer got to this black soldier.

He jokes about the girl he saw on the motorcycle, about getting too old to chase the women, about his childhood in Canada and his life in New York as the conductor on the subway. The first time you hear these stories they are interesting. After hearing them repeated for months you start to get tired of them. But, if we don't see Mac for a few days, we miss the stories, long for them like a security blanket that tells us he is all right, or at least ok.

Alzheimer's is a terrible disease for both the person with a memory that doesn't work very well anymore, and the people who share life with the victim. In many ways those who love or care about someone with this dementia are as much victims as the one whose mind is like an old string of Christmas lights, with first one bulb going out, then another, then another. It forces us to come to terms with what we expect of other people, how we function with them when part of their mind is misplaced.

Mac takes childish delight in the Christmas lights strung along the eaves of the homes and about the yards throughout the neighborhood. After the holidays each year, he will gather the discarded strings of lights from the garbage cans and spend days testing, replacing bulbs and wrapping them on pieces of cardboard. He stores them in boxes on the shelves of his garage. Next year he'll give them to neighbors who don't have lights on their houses. He is truly enchanted by the lights, by the light of the moment.

He may not remember your name, or what car you used to drive him to the Chevron Station to get his lottery tickets, or the Blake's Lotta Burger to get something for dinner, but he willingly gives you the little treasures he picks up along the streets and sidewalks of his Rio Rancho neighborhood. To some they are junk, but they have come to mean something far more significant than a magnet for the fridge, or a tiny discarded doll for the little girl next door. His mind may not make all the connections it once did, but he is still capable of teaching us all a lesson in humanity.

As Christmas day approaches, we again contemplate what would be a good and proper gift for this man who has lived through so much, been a survivor at war and life, who can no longer drive, whose aging legs still carry him but with no small measure of discomfort, even if they won't take him as far as they did a couple years ago.

Among his favorite foods are corned beef hash, TV dinners and ice cream. One has to wonder, with a diet like this, how he has remained sufficiently thin and active to celebrate his ninetieth birthday.

The annual question becomes, "What can we give Mac for Christmas this year?" We could give him a junk food basket, complete with our special homemade gingerbread cookies. But this, except for the cookies, is everyday fare that doesn't speak at all of this special season, or of his ability to be enchanted by the moment.

Perhaps a stocking full of lottery tickets would be just the thing. But, it's a part of the gambler's instinct to play the game themselves, to beat their own odds. The joy of gambling is in the undying hope, the personal commitment, investment and risk made all by yourself. How can we deny him that independence, that thrill?

Cash would be something he can use, the universal gift card. But, to give him money that will be spent tomorrow, after all recollection of its source has faded, seems to be a shallow gift, more to answer our need to give something, but without the thought and effort that would make it really meaningful.

He came to our house late this afternoon. "Boy! Sure did get dark early," he said as he put his bag of cans down outside the door. "I don't suppose you have something warm to drink, do you?" he asked as the dogs greeted him with the enthusiasm only dogs can show. They led him to the familiar chair while we heated his traditional drink.

We know that in the dark he can't find his way home. The street signs don't help because he often can't recall the street where he lives. After a few minutes to relax and share a story for the thousandth time, we ask, "Mac, it's cold out there. Can we drive you home?"

Of course he agrees and we load his bag of cans, often smelling of stale beer, in the trunk and deliver him to the relative safety of his home, his ailing wife and their niece who is undergoing chemotherapy treatments.

Traveling the six blocks to his home, we pass numerous houses and yards with multitudes of lights. The childish delight returns. We hear no sad words about the pain of aging, no comments about how difficult it is to be aware of the gradual disintegration of your mind. How often he laments, "I just can't seem to remember any more." But none of these thoughts enter his head as he lives in the moment of twinkling lights in all the brilliant colors one can imagine, even when he can't remember their names anymore.

We are living with the shortest days of the year. The early demise of the sun confuses him, as it does most of us. We are much like the plants that need the sunshine to live and grow. If we don't get enough light, we suffer both physically and mentally. Those among us with Seasonal Affective Disorder (SAD) experience depression, and are more likely to fall victim to the germs and viruses floating around in the gloom and darkness of the short winter days.

Even New Mexico feels the creeping darkness of the winter solstice. But we have our lights for the season. From hilltop and mountain side we can look down on our city lights, these beacons of life and community.

During this season of long nights and cloudy skies we celebrate the birth of a child born under the bright light of a star. We welcome anew each year, that child who was, is and ever will be, a guiding light of peace, a beacon of compassion, a soft illumination for the pathway to the ultimate mystery. This is the season of light, not darkness.

Perhaps we need the dark clouds and lengthy night sky to prepare us all for the brilliance of the sun on the new snow. How can we see the stars without the blue-black sky? How can we see the goodness that lives within each heart without the darkness of the evening news? How can we treasure the powerful light that resides in the smile of every child, without the frown found on harried adults? How could we free our spirits to be enchanted by the light, if that light didn't contrast with something else within us?

To other faiths, this is a Festival of Lights. There is the piling of wood for a great bonfire for some, while for others it's the simple lighting of a lamp. In the darkest of places, the glow of a distant Aurora Borealis can be found. These are not just symbolic flames. They illuminate the spirit within us. They truly enchant all of us willing to set aside the heavy burdens of yesterday and tomorrow and live in the moment.

Mac lives very much in the moment. He is one who can be totally enchanted by the lights of the season. Perhaps the best gift we can give him is a ride beyond his neighborhood, to be enchanted by the light of the season. We think of gifts in terms of how much should we spend? How long will it last? Does it make memories?

But, so often, the best gifts require no sacrifice and are of the moment. We can give a smile, and it will be returned. We can give a kind word that tells someone we care. We can give the gift of a moment of our time to listen, even if the story has been told many times before. We can all be enchanted by these gifts; the gestures, words and moments are all bright, colorful lights that illuminate the spirit of humanity, reflect the love of both the Creator and all creation.

As we age, our world becomes smaller and smaller. As elders, our existence diminishes, from community to neighborhood, from neighborhood to block, then to house, then to room. The contact with others also becomes more and more limited, until there is nothing, no one left.

This year we will give Mac the simple gift of a trip among the lights, beyond his neighborhood. His gift will be the simple gift of momentary enchantment. The words of wonder, the eyes wide with childish delight, the chuckle at the characters he sees moving on a rooftop, and the smile of one truly enchanted will be his gift to us, as we all treasure the sparkling beauty of the moment, a moment shared.

The Gift of the Healing Earth

Not all children dream of computer games and Barbie dolls, skateboards and bicycles. For some children Christmas is about someone else, the gifts not bought with money but purchased with love. Please join little Trudie in her journey for such a gift.

Part 1: Grandfather's cough

Grandfather coughed again and little Trudie could feel his pain in her lungs. The old man reached out with his frail hand and touched her head. The breathing was difficult, but at least the pain subsided enough to allow a smile to form. He drew enough breath to speak again, words that Trudie could hear but not understand.

"We are the people of the earth," he almost whispered, then paused, seeking sufficient breath to continue. "We have brought pain to our Mother. We have cut into her belly and left great scars."

Trudie struggled to understand, although she had heard the words many times before. It seemed that Grandfather was angry and sad at the same time. He was also racked with guilt, as terrible as the spasms of pain that assaulted his lungs.

She knew that he had been a miner. She had heard the stories Mamma told of him coming home with the yellow mud on his shoes and clothes. She remembered also the stories one old Grandmother told before she walked with the white dog to another place. When she had been angry, she would spit and call the uranium miners "worms feeding on the flesh of their Mother the Earth." This Trudie didn't understand either. But she knew that somehow Grandfather's cancer was eating his lungs, just like the miners ate the flesh of Mother Earth.

It's difficult for any six year old child to understand all of this. It's even more difficult for a six year old child with what the doctors called Fetal Alcohol Syndrome. Understanding was difficult, as was her speech, and memory. Why would her people dig holes in the Earth? What did that have to do with Grandpa's lungs? But she knew that Grandfather was hurting and all she wanted to do in the whole wide world was make him feel better, ease his pain, see again the joy in his eyes as he told her stories while they sat beside the fireplace and inhaled the smoke of pinon and juniper.

She patted his arm, "I'll find a way to make you better, Grandpa. I promise." She smiled, but couldn't stop the tears that formed in the corners of her eyes. "That will be my Christmas gift to you."

She sat with him until he fell asleep. The soft sound of the oxygen flowing through the tube into his nose, the uneven rhythm of his shallow breathing made Trudie uncomfortable. She turned on the TV and after the cartoons was a short information piece about a place called the Santuario de Chimayo. It said that many believed that the soil from this chapel could heal people. She thought long on this, even after the cartoons returned, her thoughts were on the earth of this place she had never heard of before.

Could it be that this was what Grandfather needed? Mamma worked at ACL, the Acoma, Canoncito, Laguna Hospital, but they couldn't heal him from the curse of the mines and the yellow dust. She turned the TV off, added another piece of wood to the fire and took her coat from the peg by the door. She started to leave, then turned and went to Grandfather, still sleeping in his old recliner. She gently kissed his cheek. Then, smiling with the confidence of childhood, she left the house and started the long walk down the hill to the church. She would talk to Padre Esteban about this place called Chimayo.

The elderly padre was closing the door when she arrived at the old adobe church. He invited her inside and encouraged more heat from the fire in the fireplace of his office. He listened attentively as she explained her need to get to Chimayo.

"Grandfather says that we are People-of-the-Earth. They said on the TV that it is the earth of the chapel at a place called Chimayo that heals people. That's why I must get to this place. I want to give Grandfather some of this soil for Christmas. It will heal him."

She spoke with such earnestness, such sincere conviction that Padre Esteban had to respect her faith. After all, it was a faith greater than his was now. He had lived long, seen much, and now, in these, his declining years, doubt was beginning to enter his mind. His faith had been challenged and questions were left unanswered. He smiled at this innocent child, struggling to put her words into sentences, but so enthralled with the desire to heal her grandfather. She was doomed to disappointment. There was no way that any sort of healing miracle was going to cure the cancer that was devouring his lungs. "Perhaps this is the true price we all pay for faith," he whispered to himself as stood and went to the cabinet beside the sink, "disappointment, sorrow and failure; a terrible price to pay."

He made her a cup of hot cocoa. Then, as she sipped the hot, sweet beverage, he tried to explain that Chimayo was a place of the annual pilgrimage on Good Friday, the day we reflect on the death of the physical Christ, not Christmas, the day we celebrate his birth.

"But," she spoke so fast that her words tripped over each other trying to keep up with her mind, "But, the TV showed piles of crutches from people who could walk again." She stared into his eyes, begging him to believe as strongly as she did.

10

Unfortunately, he could not call forth the faith of a child. His heart was too filled with the memories of prayers unanswered, good people suffering and dying, and his failure to prevent, to heal, to make things better for these people he had come to serve.

"Where is this place?" she asked after another sip of the hot chocolate. "I want to go there. I have to go there. I have to get some of that soil for Grandpa. Can't you help me?" she pleaded.

"It is a long way from here," he sighed, the sense of failure rising from the pit of his stomach again, choking him.

"Is it near Albuquerque?" she asked.

"Much farther," he replied, "farther than Santa Fe, almost as far as Taos."

This meant nothing to Trudie as she drained the last of the sweet liquid from the coffee mug, then licked the few drops flowing down the side. "Thank you," she said as she stood and started for the door. "Will you pray for Grandfather?"

It was cold, with a west wind denying the warmth of the afternoon sun. She walked from the church to the railroad tracks before anyone came down the road. Simon stopped the old pickup and pushed the door open. "Need a ride?" he asked as he tucked the empty beer cans under the seat.

"Thank you," she smiled as she climbed in and struggled with the seat belt.

"Where you headed?" he asked as they neared the Sky City Casino.

She looked at him, wrinkled her nose at the smell of beer and answered, "I need to go to Chimayo to get some of the soil to heal Grandfather."

He whistled as he pulled into the parking lot at the casino. "I gotta go to work now. You might want to get a ride home. It's gonna get dark soon." And with that he was out of the truck and walking toward the back door.

She walked across the street to the McDonald's beyond the gas pumps. Once inside, she sat in one of the booths and watched the people coming and going. For a brief moment she was afraid and wanted to go home, but then, in her mind, she could see Grandpa coughing and she knew what she had to do.

It was the elderly white lady that noticed her sitting alone. She walked over and asked, "Are you hungry? Would you like a hamburger?"

In a matter of minutes Trudie was enjoying a Fun Meal and a Coke while she explained to the lady why it was she had to get to the Chimayo chapel.

The lady's hearing was not very good and she thought Trudie said she was trying to get home to Chimayo after visiting her grandfather here at Acomita. "I'm on my way to Taos to visit some of my friends for Christmas. I can drop you off at Chimayo. I think it's on the way."

It wasn't until they were on the interstate highway that the old lady introduced herself. "I'm so sorry. I didn't even tell you my name, did I?"

Trudie nodded but didn't have time to put the words together to answer before the lady continued, "My name is Angeline Hildeggard. I was once a professor of European history, but they tell me I have Alzheimer's now and they want me to teach in an adult day care in Albuquerque. I don't have time for that. I have to get to Africa before Christmas and that's a long way to drive. Would you like to go to Africa?"

"No Ma'am. I just need to get to Chimayo."

They drove through the night, Trudie sleeping while Angeline stayed awake by playing music very loud on the radio of the well maintained 1989 Chrysler Imperial. It was past midnight when they pulled off I-25 and into a gas station with a snack center and several booths. Trudie followed Angeline into the restroom and then to the snack counter. Without asking, the old lady poured a cup of White Chocolate Cappuccino for her, picked up an egg salad sandwich and a bag of cookies.

They were sitting at the table sharing the sandwich when Angeline screamed, "You're nothing but a child. You shouldn't be drinking coffee. Bad girl!" She stood and without another word, walked out the door and drove off.

The clerk noticed the little girl sitting alone, sobbing, and walked over to the booth, cell phone in hand, 911 on her fingertips.

Part 2: Nun in blue jeans

Sister Anne didn't look like a nun. She looked like a teenager on her way to a high school event. She wore a blue sweatshirt with glittering stars painted on it and faded blue jeans with frayed cuffs. Her auburn hair was in a ponytail and she had an MP-3 player hooked on her belt. In her left hand was a pink overnight case, while her right hand struggled to maintain control of a folder with sheets of paper spilling out.

She stood at Trudie's booth for a moment before speaking. She was waiting for the little girl to look up from the plate of "chili cheese fries" the waitress had placed before her after making a phone call. Finally Trudie's eyes met Sister Anne's and she smiled weakly. Then she remembered her manners and offered to share her fries with the young lady.

"Hi, I'm Sister Anne," she said as she sat across the table and took one of the fries in her fingers. "MayLeene called me and said that you were unhappy and might be lost."

Trudie studied the nun's eyes for a moment before answering. "Could you tell me which way is Chimayo?" Then she waited for an answer.

Sister Anne leaned back with a puzzled look on her face. "Why would a little girl like you want to go to the Santuario de Chimayo a week before Christmas?"

"My grandfather is sick from the mining at Mount Taylor." She paused and studied the nun's face again. She couldn't read letters and numbers, but she could read faces pretty well. When it appeared that this nun didn't understand, she continued, "I saw on TV about the earth that heals and I want to get some for Grandfather for Christmas." It all made perfect sense to this little girl, but still the nun seemed not to comprehend.

With one of the sheets of paper on the table and pen in hand, she began asking questions. "What is your name?"

She consumed two more greasy fries, then licked the cheese sauce from her fingers before answering, "Trudie."

"Your last name?" Sister Anne asked, pen poised.

"I 'on't know." Trudy was looking almost scared and now was refusing to make eye contact.

"Where are you from?"

There was silence. Then she leaned forward and answered in as an adult a voice as a six year old could muster, "Africa." She nodded her head and studied Sister Anne's face to see if this satisfied her. Obviously it didn't.

"Aren't you Pueblo?" the nun was now frowning. "You look Pueblo."

"No. Bad guys captured me when I was just a baby and stole me from my African family, and my grandfather rescued me. He's a war chief. He's big and mean. He beat the bad guys up and we went back home."

Sister Anne was trying to follow this very imaginative story, but she was also studying the child's eyes very carefully. She wrote on the paper, "Fetal Alcohol Syndrome? Either runaway or abandoned."

"Want to listen to some music?" she asked Trudie as she motioned to the waitress. She ordered hot chocolate and green chile burgers for each of them.

Trudie sipped the hot chocolate and asked, "Will you help me get to Chimayo?"

"Yes," Sister Anne responded with a smile that Trudie knew was a lie. "But first I want you to come to the chapel with me and get a good night's sleep. We can start out early in the morning."

After the only remaining evidence of the green chile burgers was a few crumbs and a couple grease spots, they went to the register to pay. While the nun was fumbling though her purse for the change, Trudie wandered over to the candy rack. When she saw that the nun was occupied, she slipped out the door and ran to an old battered pickup that looked like Simon's. She opened the door and climbed in. Then she scrunched down on the floor so Sister Anne couldn't see her.

She cautiously peeked out the window as the nun ran out the door calling, "Trudie! Trudie!" Then she was on her cell phone. In minutes the police car was there. Trudie whispered to herself, "I was bad and she called 911. The police came to get me. I got to keep quiet."

The old man came out of the convenience store and opened the truck door. He threw the bag with the milk and a box of donuts on the seat and put the key in the ignition as the police officer walked over to the truck.

"We seem to have a lost little girl, about five or six. Probably Indian. Seen any kids in the last hour or so?" The officer shined his flashlight on the passenger seat as he spoke.

13

"There was a kid inside with a young lady. Didn't see her come out though." He started the engine and, as he was shifting into reverse, added, "I'll keep my eye out. If I see her, I'll let you guys know. Merry Christmas." With that he backed out of the parking space and eased the old truck onto the road. It was starting to snow. Big flakes danced in front of the headlights and silently struck the windshield.

It was when the old man leaned over to put a CD in the slot that he saw the little girl huddled on the floor. He whistled and pulled off onto the side of the now almost snow covered road, just as an old John Denver song, *"Christmas for Cowboys,"* began playing.

Tears flowed down Trudie's cheeks as she sniffled. "Please don't hurt me," she said between sobs. Memories from somewhere in her past were haunting her and the fear was making it difficult to breathe.

When he turned the cab light on, she studied his face for a moment, then smiled and wiped away the last of the tears. She recognized the white whiskers and the long white hair that flowed from under the tattered and stained leather cowboy hat. The red plaid flannel jacket confirmed her first impression.

"WOW!" she exclaimed as she climbed onto the seat and worked at securing the seatbelt. "Padre Esteban told me to pray. I did, and it worked." The smile was so broad that she could hardly speak.

Part 3: Filling the Medicine Bag

"Are you going to Chimayo?" she became very serious as she asked with a faith she feared was being tested.

The old man glanced away from the headlights on the road to study this child's face. She seemed small, too small to speak with such conviction. His first inclination was to turn around, return to the convenience store and contact the police. But her eyes were pleading for help. How could he say no?

"Why do you want to go to Chimayo, Child?" he asked as he started back out onto the highway. Then he added, "Where are your parents?"

She lowered her head and muttered, "Mamma's in jail. The police got her." She paused and wiped the new, hot tears from her eyes. "I live with Gramma and Grandpa. Grandfather can't breathe. That's why I need to go to Chimayo." Secure in the conviction that she had explained her situation, she leaned back in the seat and, with her eyes lowered, waited for his response.

His eyes were back on the snow covered road. He asked her where she was from.

She hesitated to answer him. Finally she almost whispered, "Acoma." After a long silence she added, "Grandfather was a miner and got the yellow dust sickness. That's why he can't breathe. His lungs are dying and he needs the soil from Chimayo. The TV said it would make him better. That's what I want to give him for Christmas."

14

It all seemed so logical in her little mind. The old man now had tears in his eyes. He stopped the old pickup in the middle of the road, unbuckled his seat belt, reached over and took the child in his arms. Her tears were dried by the soft white beard.

They were silent for a momentary eternity. Finally he released her, smiled and tried to speak, but he choked on the words and, as the old John Denver CD began playing *"Silent Night,"* he turned around in the middle of the now slippery road and, in what was now a sincere snow storm, slowly drove several miles back the way they had come. In the heavy snow it was almost impossible to see the rusted old sign. When the headlights caught the black letters, he almost slid through the intersection and onto the semi-paved road.

She was now sound asleep. He struggled to navigate the snow covered road, winding up and down hills, navigating sharp curves and slippery patches of ice. He was very tired himself but he wanted to reach his destination before she woke up.

The snow was letting up as the first hint of dawn, the faint light of a promise Father Sun made every evening that he would return, glowed pink over the hillsides to the east. They pulled into the 24 hour gas station and up to the pump. He got out and went around to the passenger door. She was still sleeping when he took her in his arms and carried her inside. The lady filling the coffee maker turned as the bell on the door jangled to announce their presence.

"Madre Dios," she exclaimed, "what have you got there?"

"Think she may need to visit the restroom and get her face washed," he said as Lupe took the child into her arms.

She studied the child's face. Then she turned to the old man. "Is this the little girl they were talking about on the radio last night?" Before he had a chance to respond, she continued, "They are afraid she might be lost in the snow, or maybe was kidnaped. I'd better call the police."

He touched her arm, "Please don't. We have to go to Chimayo." He lowered his voice and almost whispered, "Her grandfather's dying and she wants the soil as a Christmas gift for him. We can't deny a faith like that."

Lupe took her to the restroom while the old man finished filling the coffee pots. In a few minutes they returned, face washed and hair combed.

When Trudie saw him, she smiled and turned to Lupe, "He's taking me to Chimayo. I'm gonna get the earth there. When Grandfather heals he's gonna help the Earth Mother heal too."

After a breakfast and a refueling that Lupe refused to accept payment for, Trudie buckled herself in the seat and the old man got behind the wheel. Just as they pulled onto the road, the church bells rang in the distance, the sun was just peaking over the snow crested hills to the east. Trudie began singing in a language the old man could not understand, but he knew within his heart that this little girl was praying. When he began to sing along with her, she smiled and touched his arm.

As they crested another hill and descended around another sharp curve, she could see far off on the next hill the Santuario de Chimayo, just like she had seen on TV. The old man pulled off the road and silenced the engine. They sat looking at the chapel and the buildings that surrounded it. The chapel seemed to be glowing in the crisp morning sun.

Finally, the old man spoke. "You know they say that the healing was first reported in 1816, but the Tewa Indians knew this was a sacred place long before that. Today they call it the Lourdes of America, but its story goes back much farther."

There was a long silence where both the old man and the little girl were lost deep within their thoughts. He was wondering if there was anyone in the whole world who would go this far for him, would care enough to endure the cold and solitude. Tears formed in the corners of his eyes.

She sat staring at the chapel. It wasn't the grand structure she was expecting. It looked very common, much like the churches on the rez. It was in need of repair. The adobe walls were weathered and worn. The wood on the bell tower was paint starved and warped. She was wondering if this was really the right place. There was a sign, but she couldn't read. Perhaps this was a trick the old man was playing on her. She crossed her hands and looked up to the sky as she began praying to the Mother of Jesus. She prayed that this was the right place. Then she prayed that she would be able to find the soil. As the tears filled her eyes and overflowed, she prayed that she would be able to find her way back to Acomita in time to save Grandfather.

He started the old truck and eased up the hill and into the parking lot. Now that they were closer, she could see that it was exactly like the pictures on TV. Yes! This truly was Chimayo. The snow was deep but many footsteps had gone before them so, even in her sneakers, without boots, she was able to keep her feet almost dry. At the cross in the plaza the old man knelt and crossed himself. She watched him. Then she repeated his gestures. He stood and took her hand in his.

When they entered the door, on the right was a place to put money. She was concerned because she didn't even think about paying admission. The old man took his wallet from his pocket and removed the last two dollar bills it contained. He started to put them in the container, then paused. He handed her one of them, then folded the one he held and dropped it into the slot. She watched carefully as he did this, and did exactly as he had done. They entered the rustic chapel and found space in the last of the old, handcrafted pews. There was no service, only a tour guide explaining the history of this unique place of miracles.

Trudie listened intently, trying to understand every word, but some of what was said confused her. Finally the guide pointed to the door at the left. "Through that door you will find the miraculous soil of the Santuario de Chimayo. Please proceed quickly through the hallway, and watch your step as you enter the room. We ask that you take only a small amount of the soil. Keep your prayers brief. Then, proceed up the ramp. As you exit, note all the crutches, even wheelchairs, and other articles of infirmity, left as proof of the miracles that have occurred here."

As they entered the dimly lit room, people were scooping up soil and filling plastic bags, mason jars and ornate bottles. While the old man watched, Trudie knelt and opened her medicine bag. She carefully scooped up one small handful of the precious soil and dumped it into the leather pouch. When she stood, she saw the chipped green Oxygen tank, discarded along with the crutches.

She smiled. As they went through the doorway, the sun burst from behind a cloud, bathing them in its light and warmth. Trudie looked into the old man's face. She reached up and touched his snow white beard. "Thank you," she said as they crossed the little plaza and walked past the rustic Nativity set up under the junipers. "This is going to be the best Christmas ever."

They went back to the old truck and, as she was climbing in, it struck her that now she had to find her way back home. This thought put her on the edge of panic. Huge, hot tears formed in her eyes and began to flow, encouraged by deep sobs. Again he took her in his arms and held her tightly. Between sobs and coughs she asked him how she was going to get home.

He hadn't even thought of this. This was his busy season. He just couldn't drive all the way to Acomita and back in time to . . . well, do all he needed to have accomplished before Christmas day.

Finally he helped her buckle up and backed out of the parking space. They slowly drove down the hill and onto one of the semi-paved roads that abound in this region of New Mexico, roads without names and numbers. He began to explain that after he dropped off the feed at the farm, they would start out for her home. He knew the way to Acomita. It was near the Sky City Casino he visited on occasion along Interstate 40. He would have to call off work, but this was more important.

She clutched the medicine bag to her heart, whispered another prayer, then fell asleep. He glanced time and again at that medicine bag, deerskin, with symbols painted on it. There was a leather tie that held it secure. It was decorated with turquoise, some other stones, a green feather and a twig of some sort.

While she slept, he navigated the roads until finally he was at the gate.

Part 4: Healing Earth

She awoke when he opened the truck door to unlatch the gate. As he drove over the cattle guard, she saw the first of the animals coming toward them. Of course, it was logical. He had to have the reindeer somewhere. That was why the back of the pickup was full of hay and bags of feed. Then the sheep came over to the truck, then three cows and two calves. She tried to sort out the logic of all this. It began to make sense. Of course, he had to have a farm for the deer. He must have cows and sheep, probably some chickens somewhere too. After all, weren't they a part of every farm?

He slowly drove up to the barn. The plump lady with gray hair came out the door of the old farmhouse. She looked just like the picture in the Christmas book Grandfather read to her last year when he could breathe. All of a sudden, she missed Grandfather very much. The tears began to flow again, but when the deer came up to her side of the truck and licked the window, she had to laugh. She struggled to wind the window down, took one of the donuts from the bag on the seat, and offered it to him. As this creature enjoyed the treat, she patted it on the head and cautiously touched the antlers. They were much smaller than she remembered from the pictures in the book.

The old man and his wife were unloading the bags of feed and the bales of hay. Where were the elves? Shouldn't they be helping?

Soon she was sitting at the kitchen table with a plate of scrambled eggs smothered in green chile in front of her. While she ate, the old man was talking on the phone. "Yes, I know this is the week before Christmas, but this is important," he said. There was a long pause. "I have to take her to Acoma." Then there was another, longer pause. "Yes. I'll be back for the evening shift. Yes, I'll even bring Prancer."

There was a long pause again. Finally, he said with anger in his voice, "If you think you can find another Santa with a real beard and a herd of deer the week before the big day, go ahead and try. I'm telling you this little girl is more important." Then he placed the phone on the desk and turned to his wife, "I'll need some coffee." As he reached for his heavy red coat hanging on the peg by the door, he turned and added, "I'm going to put Prancer in the trailer. Do we have a new coat for her?" With that he winked and smiled at Trudie and was out the door.

In a matter of minutes he was back. Trudie was washed, teeth brushed and hair combed. She was wearing a pretty pink snow suit and almost new boots. His wife was wearing a coat and her red felt Lady Stetson.

"I'm going along," she announced. "You might need to take a nap on the way back to Santa Fe if you're going to work this evening."

They all climbed into the old pickup and were soon on the road. While the old lady sang Christmas songs in both English and Spanish, Trudie fell asleep. They were on I-25 before she awakened. Snow was falling and the junipers on the hillsides were beautiful with their fresh snow cover, like frosting on a Christmas cookie.

Soon they reached the 'Big I' in Albuquerque. This is the intersection of I-25 and I-40. It was another hour before they reached the Sky City Casino and turned onto the road to Acomita. Trudie became very quiet. She pointed to the road they needed to take to her grandma's house. Then she clutched the medicine bag in her hands, closed her eyes and prayed again. She prayed so hard that tears flowed. When she opened her eyes they were almost to the old house that was home to her, Grandma and Grandfather.

As they made the turn onto the street where she lived, a police car approached from the other direction. It followed them into the yard. Grandma opened the door just as the old lady got out of the pickup and helped Trudie onto the familiar ground. Trudie ran to Grandma, just as the policeman came over to them and looked down at her. "Are you ok?" he said, obviously worried.

"Yes." Trudie answered, afraid of this tribal officer. She grabbed Grandma's hand and held on tightly.

Grandma took her granddaughter in her arms and hugged her. "Where have you been?" she asked as she looked from Trudie to the elderly couple standing beside the truck.

Trudie pointed to the old man with the white beard and his wife in the red Stetson. "Santa took me to Chimayo to get the soil to heal Grandfather." She paused to study her grandmother's face. "Is . . . is Grandfather ok?" Now she looked frightened. Her lip quivered. "I got it right here," she said as she held the medicine bag up for Grandma to see.

The Priest, Father Esteban, pulled into the yard and somberly walked over to them. "I got here as quickly as I could," he said as he looked at the strange assemblage in the yard, a tribal cop, an elderly white couple that looked like, well, like Mr. and Mrs. Santa, and Trudie, back home, safe and sound. "Is he . . . is he still . . . ?"

Grandma put Trudie down and led the priest inside without another word. Trudie's eyes opened wide as she looked up into the sky and cried as loudly as she could "NOOOOOOOOO!" Then she ran into the house. There in the old recliner was Grandfather. She held the medicine bag containing the sacred earth in her hand. Grandfather opened his eyes at the sound of his granddaughter's voice. His breathing was very weak, very painful. He smiled, and that took all the strength he had. He closed his eyes again.

"I went to Chimayo and got you the healing earth. It will make you well. Then you can heal the Earth Mother." She spoke with the simple faith, and logic, of a child.

As Father Esteban took the medicine bag from her hands and prayed over it, the Medicine man entered the room. The tribal officer whispered what was happening as the priest opened the medicine bag and took a pinch of the brown earth in his fingers. He made the sign of the cross over Grandfather's chest and touched the dying man's lips with the sacred, healing earth, the earth of faith, the simple faith of a child.

The medicine man took the bag from the priest's hand and stepped out the door. In the yard he held it up to the sun, even though it was hidden behind a snow cloud. Even when it couldn't be seen, all knew that the sun was still there. It was the same with the Creator, the one who makes miracles from the faith of even a small child.

He returned to Trudie's grandfather and spoke in almost a whisper, in Keres, the traditional language. As he spoke, he also took a pinch of the earth in his fingers and touched the dying man with it, touched his closed eyes and his chest, his heart and lastly, his lips. The two holy men prayed to the Creator, known by different names, but still the same Creator. Trudie took her medicine bag from the hand of the medicine man and placed it on Grandfather's chest.

It was several minutes later that Grandfather opened his eyes and smiled weakly. When he saw Trudie, he smiled for a second time and motioned with his hand for her to come nearer. She hugged him and started babbling about her trip to Chimayo and how Santa had helped her get the healing Earth that would make him better so that he could heal the Earth's wounds from the mining.   The Medicine man looked at this little girl, awed by the determination she possessed at such an early age. Father Esteban crossed himself as tears formed in his eyes and he felt a special warmth in his heart. He marveled at the faith of this child, a faith so much stronger than his own. In the recliner, a dying man smiled at the wisdom and faith of his granddaughter. He was so proud of her. Something within his heart told him that he could not let her down. Nor could he fail in her vision of him healing the wounds of the Earth Mother.

With her limited understanding, she asked Grandfather if he would let her help him heal the Earth Mother's wounds. In school they called her slow, stupid, even mean, but here she was a gift. Both priest and Medicine man could see her gifts.

The medicine man looked around for the elderly couple who had helped Trudie in her quest for the healing earth of Chimayo and her journey back to Grandfather. They were gone. The old battered pickup was gone. But on the porch was a box of Christmas cookies and a note that said, "Thank you Trudie. Thank you for carrying the spirit of Christmas in your heart. It is said that a child shall show us the way. One of these children was born over two thousand years ago. Another is now six and inspires us all to live our faith and share our wisdom."

Trudie was convinced that she had been helped by Mr. & Mrs. Santa Claus, but the reality was that they were just farmers who happened to raise several exotic species of deer as a hobby. He happened to have a real white beard and was able to pick up a little spending money during the Christmas season working part time as a department store Santa in Santa Fe.

Miracles do happen. They take the involvement and commitment of friends, love of family, and faith of strangers. It was months before Grandfather was able to return the oxygen tanks to ACL and walk with his cane around the yard. It was spring before he rode with Trudie and Grandma to visit Mount Taylor and speak to the sacred mountain.

Was his healing the result of the healing earth of Chimayo? Was it the faith of a child? Was it the cooperation of a diverse group of people who became involved by coincidence, or are there no coincidences? Perhaps it is when we think of others that miracles happen. Perhaps this is what Christmas is really about, letting go and letting ourselves be a part of the miracle of the season.

When there was talk of uranium mining again, it was Grandfather, accompanied by his granddaughter, who spoke so forcefully, with such simple logic and profound truth about his Christmas gift and the power of the faith of a child. "With this courage and wisdom we can all stand up and say 'NO!!' to those who would sell our Mother, who would trade the blessings of our sacred pollen for the curse of the demon's yellow dust."

Perhaps Christmas is really the opportunity to celebrate our better selves, be the gift, even when some call us damaged, or a throw away child, we are all still a gift. Together, we are a miracle, the real miracle of Christmas.

For the Love of Luminita

We were working on an article on the unique local histories and traditions that are a part of our Southwestern small towns. This research had taken us to dozens of communities, villages that were clinging to their past in the dust of the deserts and high plateau. We had been to mountainside towns accessible only by dirt roads, occupied by only a family or two.

So many of these communities were anachronisms, leftovers from a culture that was no more. To be frankly honest, we were getting bored with this process of interviewing the occupants of almost ghost towns. It was depressing. We wanted to get home for the Christmas season, but the deadline was January 25th and we had to get all these visits out of the way. One of the last places on our list was a valley town called La Paz.

We arrived there late in the afternoon on December 20th. Snow flurries falling from a dark, sunless sky added to our depression and lack of enthusiasm. There was only one place to eat and that was the lunch counter at the Phillips 66 gas station. We chose the booth closest to the door, ordered green chile burgers and coffee. From the window we could watch the activity that was going on at the Chapel across the street, beyond the quaint and crumbling little plaza.

Our waitress was in her mid-forties, pleasantly plump, with curly black hair and a smile that warmed the entire room. It soon became obvious that she was mentally slow. After she took our order to the kitchen, she returned with the coffee. I asked her what was happening at the church. She told us they were getting ready for la Posada and the festival of The Love of Luminita. She seemed almost embarrassed as she answered our questions.

After our meal, we braved the cold to cross the street and begin our interviews. We found the mayor, Diego de Aguilar, in the cluster of people building a life size creche. He was smoking a cigar. The foul smoke floated through the air as he paused in his labors and led us to a park bench under the winter bare branches of a massive cottonwood. There we all sat as he related the following events from the history of the village of La Paz. This is the story he told us.

Christmas is a season with more symbols of love, more expressions of giving, caring and sharing than any other time of the year. For a few days it seems that all humanity can actually live in peace and harmony, differences and prejudices can be put away, and the light within all is given the freedom to shine.

21

This had been the tradition of the village of La Paz in the shadow of the Sangre de Cristo Mountains. Here the fewer than 200 residents lived a quiet life. The year was 1955 and there wasn't a television in the community, only a few of the homes had a telephone and many were without electricity. Life was simple, but there was a comfort in the close-knit community that the city folk down in Santa Fe and Albuquerque had forgotten. La Paz was a town with a plaza where people gathered at the fountain, sat on the benches, smelled the roses and engaged in relaxed conversation.

The smell of cigar smoke would waft through the plaza, emanating from the shade of the cottonwoods. These were already ancient trees, spreading their protective arms over the benches and tables, reaching up to the sky with heart-shaped leaves in constant motion, waving at the sun. Within the branches could be found at various times jays, magpies, ravens, doves, wrens and mockingbirds, robins, warblers and chickadees. The squirrels would chatter, beg and entertain the children.

In the shade of these majestic trees, most of the important work of the village mayor was conducted. Juan Baptiste de Aguilar had earned the position of mayor by living 77 years; that, and being the best domino player in La Paz. Dominos was the sport of choice of the men in this and many of the other communities in small town New Mexico. It was at the tables with the ivories spread before them that ideas were formed, issues were discussed, and decisions made.

The seasons of La Paz were marked by the scents carried in the air. There was always the faint, somehow comforting odor of the cigars and pipes, but it was the fragrance of the lilacs that told the children they could go barefoot, told their mothers to clean house and plant the garden, told the men to clean the acequias, till the fields and repeat the cycle of their fathers and fathers before them. The roses releasing their sweet aroma from the courtyard of the Chapel de Santa Maria de Guadalupe told the town that summer was at hand, that the hustle and energy of spring was to be replaced with the slower pace of summer. If spring was a time to plant dreams, then summer was surely the season to nurture those dreams. The dreams of the children splashing in the irrigation water flowing through the acequias, and the dreams of the farmers were verified in the faces of the old men playing dominos, and the scent of cigar smoke in the shade of the cottonwoods.

The intoxicating fragrance of chiles roasting in the metal drums marked the approach of autumn. The season of harvest is the time to return from the idyll of summer to the discipline of putting by, preparing for the coming of winter. It was the fragrance from the kitchens where canning was a family affair, from the orchards where apples were harvested, and the cider press where piles of discarded pulp ripened in the autumn sun. Mingled with this was the ever present smoke from Juan's cigars, a comforting and reassuring sign that all was right in La Paz.

Juan Baptiste was fond of saying, "spring, summer and fall are all seasons when we look ahead, they are the times of the year when we work toward tomorrow. Winter is the favorite season of an old man, for that is when we live for today, with bittersweet thoughts of yesterday."

Winter is the smell of pinon smoke from the fireplaces carried on the crisp, clear, cold wind that blows down from the mountains. "It is a time in the cycle of our earthly existence when we are to relax and reflect on our purpose and our God," Juan would proclaim at the feast of Thanksgiving.

Still the old men would bundle themselves in heavy coats, dust the snow from the tables and play dominos. Still the smoke from the cigars carried the message that all is well.

There is a fifth season to the year that has special meaning for all, and has its own special fragrances. This fifth season touches everyone, brings out the best in all of us. The advent of Christmas in a small village is different from the coming of Christmas in a big city. In La Paz, the fragrance of baking breads, sweet treats, biscochitos, and hot cider, blend with the scent of pine and juniper boughs that decorate the homes, shops, school and chapel. It is the sweet smell of peace that marks this, our fifth season. These are the life affirming fragrances that almost overwhelm the cigar smoke from the domino players led by Mayor Juan Baptiste.

In the small town of La Paz, it was the custom the week before Christmas to engage the entire village in *la Posada*, the symbolic journey of Joseph and Mary into that other little village called Bethlehem and their search for lodging. In this procession it was stressed how cold it was and how difficult this would be for the baby soon to be born.

This procession ended at the courtyard of the chapel where the mayor and his friends along with the aging priest, Padre Pietro, had created a scenario of the birth of the infant, complete with a manger, straw, live sheep, a couple burros and an aging milk cow. Because there was no camel in La Paz, an old horse was given the honor of representing that beast of burden from a different desert, and a different time.

The people of La Paz could understand perhaps better than the people in the cities what this birth meant, because they lived daily with the desert, they tended their sheep and their fields. They may have been removed by almost two thousand years, but they were still a part of that tradition, that culture common to all people of the desert.

On Christmas Eve a doll wrapped in a Pendleton blanket was placed in this makeshift manger with great ceremony and prayers from Padre Pietro. Prayers that many felt went on far too long, but no one would criticize the good Father. Then all would enter the chapel for the Christmas eve mass. As soon as the mass was over, candles were lit all over the plaza and farilitos would line the walkways to the chapel. Music was played, bottles of wine and cider were passed around, food shared. The celebration of an entire village lit the midnight sky and filled the air with sounds of joy.

As was the case with many of these small New Mexico towns, most of the residents were Catholic Hispanos, but there were always a few Anglos and perhaps a Black family as well. Artie Feldman and his wife, Glenda, were the only Jews in La Paz. Still they were welcomed as fully as possible, shared in the festivals and in the work. Artie worked shoulder to shoulder with everyone else to clear the acequias every spring, plant the crops, help with the lambing, and defending the flocks from coyotes.

Glenda had been a nurse in Philadelphia, and shared her skill with the curanderas in times of sickness and injury. Three years after they arrived in La Paz, Glenda gave birth to their first and only child. They were so eager to be a part of this community that they gave her a name in the Hispanic tradition, Luminita, child of the light, the light of their life.

Just before Luminita was a year old, she took ill, with a high fever. Then she went into convulsions. They rushed her to the clinic, then on to the hospital in Santa Fe where she stayed for three weeks. She survived, but the fever had been too high, for too long. Lovely Luminita came home from the hospital with brain damage. The reaction of the village had been swift. They came with the great gift of sympathy, and held special prayer vigils, lit hundreds of candles and shed tears along with the parents.

Still, as Luminita grew, her inability to comprehend even the simple games of childhood made it difficult for her to be a part of the activities. As the river of time flowed and she grew from infant to toddler, then child, a distance began to grow between the Feldmans and the rest of the village. Even though they attended the chapel every Sunday and worked with the men and women of the village, they were well aware of the comments that were made behind their back, the whispered questions about what would become of Luminita, the suggestion by some that this was God's punishment for their refusal to accept Jesu Christo.

In 1955 Luminita was eight years old; if you disregard the calendar. She was mentally four years old, and possessed the smile of an angel and a simple joy in living that was a comfort to her parents, and a true gift to those willing to embrace her and open their hearts to this little girl. She had spent the afternoon helping Glenda bake their special cinnamon biscochitos. Then she collected all the candle stubs they had stored in the house for the Christmas Eve on the plaza. This would be the first year she could light candles and she had been practicing under her father's protective eye. She had even been practicing the carols with her mother so that she could join in with everyone else in singing about the birth of this baby. She took a long nap so that she could be a part of the celebration, and light candles, and sing.

"Oh, I love Christmas," she told her mother with a great big hug.

Christmas Eve in 1955 was exceptionally cold, and it was snowing as the townsfolk gathered in the plaza. There was a harsh, biting wind blowing down from the Sangre de Cristos. As each family entered the courtyard of the chapel they paused at the nativity; many knelt, other crossed themselves.

Luminita knelt like the others, but when she arose there were tears in her eyes. As they entered the chapel she looked back one more time at the doll lying in the manger, its face almost covered by the blowing snow. Several of the menfolk took the sheep and burros, the cow and the horse back to the barn, out of the cold, before they went inside.

She sang, but with less enthusiasm than Glenda had expected. Luminita helped the other children set the candles in the paper bags from the plaza to the door of the little church. Then she and the other children lit them. These farolitos were to light the way for the family of el Nino. She helped to spread the cookies on the tables.

Still, she seemed sad. Artie noticed and thought that his daughter must be cold. He gave her a big hug and wrapped his coat around her shoulders. Then he turned back to the discussion with the Mayor and Padre Peitro about it how must have been for the Jewish people living under Roman rule. Juan Baptiste even gave Artie one of his cigars and held up a candle to light it for him.

In the joy of music and the sharing of food, no one noticed that Luminita was no longer in the plaza.

It was almost midnight when a hush fell over those gathered. The whispered news spread rapidly. The music stopped. The wine bottles were set on the tables. The cookie crumbs were brushed from moustaches and cheeks.

"El Nino is missing!"

The entire population of La Paz ran to the chapel courtyard. Sure enough, the manger was empty. El Nino was gone.

"Es el diablo," several of the folks commented.

Fear filled some, while others felt anger. In the midst of this confusion, Artie and Glenda were looking for their little girl. The word soon spread that not only was the Infante stolen, but the retarded child had also been kidnaped.

A village is a family, and even if they squabble and bicker among themselves, they unite whenever one of their number is threatened. Torches were lit from the candles. As many of the men, women and children fanned out to search the homes, others ventured into the darkness surrounding the community, the cold and the now drifted snow illuminated only by the stars shining above.

It was in everyone's mind, though not a single person spoke the words. "Luminita couldn't last more than an hour in this cold." There was a desperation in the search, but behind this concern was the fear that there was evil at work. A witch or the devil had stolen both of them.

Townsfolk moved in groups for security against a force they could neither comprehend nor identify. Clusters of torches moved out of the plaza and down to the canal while others disappeared behind the chapel and up the hillside.

An hour later the groups began drifting back, cold and discouraged. It was decided to begin a house by house search. After more sips from the wine bottles, with courage renewed, the torches were ignited again. It was only a few minutes after this second search was under way that the shouting began.

"We have found el Nino!" Inez shouted as she stood at the doorway of the church. All rushed toward her and gazed inside. There on one of the old pine pews, wrapped in Arti's coat lay the doll, the symbolic Christ child. Beside the Infante lay Luminita, sound asleep.

Someone shouted, "The retarded kid took him."

An angry group rushed past Inez and began shouting. The noise awoke her. With a shriek of fear she stumbled from the pew and cowered in the corner. Several men seized her by the arms and dragged her into the courtyard. The village now became a mob. While some were rescuing the doll and preparing to return it to the manger, others were demanding punishment.

It was Mayor Juan Baptiste who finally shouted them to silence, and relit his stub of a cigar, stalling for time to think his way through this crisis. The scent of the cigar's smoke was again reassuring, calming, a call to thought rather than action.

Padre Pietro led them all in a prayer of thanks for the return of El Nino.

Then the mayor went to the cluster of angry men surrounding Artie, Glenda and Luminita in the plaza that had been filled with so much joy earlier. He knelt before the little girl and asked "Why did you do this terrible thing?"

She sniffled and tried to blink the cold tears from her eyes, "If you love God's baby, how could you leave him out in the cold?"

"But you shouldn't have stolen the doll, it wasn't yours."

"I didn't steal him. I just wanted to make him warm and comfortable." She sniffled again and continued, "Padre Pietro told us tonight that God loves us. Didn't he?"

"Yes, he did."

"And that we should love God?"

Padre Pietro entered the dialogue by nodding his agreement.

"Then how could you leave him alone in the cold, all covered with snow?"

Every year, since that Christmas Eve in 1955, La Paz has added a new tradition, called the celebration of the Love of Luminita. They have one of the children show the way of love by bringing El Nino into the chapel with them.

"Sometimes it takes the light of a child to illuminate our path," Mayor Diego de Aguilar told us. He then added that his father had been mayor in 1955.

We asked what happened to Luminita.

He pointed to the Phillips 66 station across the street. "She works as a waitress over there. Go over and wish her a Happy Hanukkah and Feliz Navidad, why don't cha."

The Story of Old Nick

So often we value an individual by the wealth and material goods accumulated, or the conquests and victories won. But the true heroes are made of better stuff. They may not be honored in the history book and statues in the park, or pictured on the currency of commerce, but they are reflected in the way we live, the way we journey through life, the way we celebrate our existence by sharing who we are, by being the gift. Old Nick was such a person. This is his story, what little we know of it; fact or fiction, myth or reality. As you read this story, perhaps Old Nick will remind you of someone you know.

The story is told when the cold winds blow, and the snow swirls and gathers on the sage and the chamisa bush. The story is told of the old man who wandered the hills and called no place home. By most folks' standards, Nick was the ultimate failure at life.

It seemed he could never hold a job for longer than it took to get to payday. He had tried prospecting, but spent most of his time sitting and watching the jays chatter and the squirrels play. Up in Santa Fe he once worked as a store clerk, but when he just outright gave Anita Ramos the cloth to make her daughter an Easter dress, it was agreed that he didn't understand merchandising. When he got a job at the cafe in Belen, he made certain that every penniless drifter got a square meal. He held that job for almost a week.

As a cowhand, he could usually last about a month before just wandering off on some personal journey. He would show up when the crops were ready for harvest, usually at a farm where help was most needed. Often he would work for a place to stay at night, a good meal and an opportunity to share stories in the evening after the work was done.

Truth be known, this was the reason most folks were glad to see Old Nick wander into town or knock at their door. He told damn good stories. Some claimed there was a great deal of distance between these tales and the truth, but this didn't diminish the interest folks had in the telling. It was by the fireplace, a cup of boiled coffee and a light flickering from the oil lamp that Nick was at his best. Here he was doing what he was born to do, talk.

In the process of sipping coffee and weaving a good story, he often helped a family over a rough spot. Sometimes it was in the story that advice was given, or problems solved. Like the time he sat in the kitchen of the Barkley's old farmhouse and talked to Art and Sarah about the need to work as a team. He told the story of a farmer who possessed two high spirited and very strong work horses. Problem was they always wanted to go off in two different directions, so little work got done and the fields were always late gettin' plowed. Then one day one of them horses came up lame and the other had to do all the work. In the week of pulling the wagon all by himself, and dragging the stone boat without any help at all, he came to appreciate the other half of the team. Ever after that time those horses pulled together. Then there weren't no stump too tough for them, no load too heavy. After that time this farmer's place was the best kept farm in the county and his crops were always prime. Every one of the neighbors spoke well of his team and his skill as a farmer.

"It was all a matter of them two horses learnin' to pull together," Old Nick said as he helped himself to a refill from the coffee pot on the stove. From that day on, Art and Sarah worked hard at helping each other instead of finding fault with the shortcomings, which they each had in abundance.

Lex Evans' boy had taken to spendin' too much time in town, not learnin' the lesson that he was a damn poor gambler, and not even very good at drinkin.' When he was told to paint the barn, he did the far side in shades of blue and green, with clouds and a bright orange sun shinin' from the corner.

It was Old Nick that hauled the wayward young man home in the back of that ancient buckboard. As they fanned the dust out of their eyes, Nick began talkin' to him about the beauty of a good life and how early morning was the most glorious time of the day, 'cept for the sunset on a day well spent.

He left him on the hillside looking out over the Estancia Valley. "Just think about the wonder of God's beauty and the good people you can see workin' at making a life in this broad valley," Nick told the young man. "I'll be back for ya, come sundown." He also left his notebook and a couple pencils, along with a canteen.

When he returned, the lad was eager to show him the pencil sketches of the patterns the fence rows made as they marched up hills and across the open spaces, of a calf following the cow as she searched for some tender spring grass, of the Alvarez family working together to plant the bean fields, and other studies of clouds, shadows and the ruins of some ancient mission called Quarai.

It wasn't that the boy was a great artist. But, on this day, as he sat alone among the junipers on the hillside, he made a great discovery. Old Nick didn't talk much on the way to the Evans farm that evening. He just listened as the lad described the world he saw in the farms and ranches spread out before him that day. For the first time in his life he had stood far enough away from himself to see the beauty around him. This is an important lesson for all of us to learn, a discovery too few make.

When Cal Silvas was laid up with the fever, Old Nick showed up late in the afternoon askin' for some hot coffee and a warm spot by the fire to spend the night. Angela, Cal's wife, welcomed him, but apologized for not having anything but some bone soup and a pot of Indian tea she was using to heal Cal. "We been without coffee for most of the month, and real food's not much more than a fond memory," she told him as he dusted the snow from his hat and coat.

He walked over to the bed where Cal lay wheezing and coughing somethin' terrible. He took a worn leather pouch from his coat pocket. "This was give to me by an Indian women over at Laguna. If I recollect right, she said this was good for just what ails you."

With that said, he asked Angela for a cup of hot water. When she brought it to him, he added a pinch of the dried leaves and twigs from the pouch. There was a fragrance of mint and something else not quite as pleasant smelling. In a few minutes, the tea had steeped and was cooled enough to drink. Within the hour Cal had stopped wheezing and was breathing much easier. Then Nick took a tin of dark brown cream from his other coat pocket and rubbed some on Cal's neck and chest.

While Cal was breathing more comfortably and Angela was adding the last of the chicos to the bone soup, Old Nick went out to tend his horse and get his things from the wagon. Neither Cal nor Angelina saw him pick up their old rifle leaning against the door frame. As the sun was setting they heard a single gunshot. A half hour later, in the silver darkness of a winter's eve, Nick opened the door and, without a word, handed Angela a venison steak. A few minutes later he returned with a bag of corn meal in his hand and a sack of pinto beans on his shoulder.

While Nick dressed out the deer he had shot, Angela prepared a feast. Angela was from the Pueblos and, as is their custom, left morsels of the food in a special bowl. They called it the "Spirit bowl" as a way of sharing with the unseen. Nick helped Cal from the bed to the table for dinner. As they all sat at the table, Nick bowed his head and thanked the Creator by all the names he knew. Then they feasted and he told stories that had been given to him by an old Indian a year ago. They talked until the fire was little more than warm coals.

By morning Cal was feeling stronger and the coughing had stopped. He was able to get to the table himself and ate a good breakfast of venison strips and corn tortillas with pintos and dried chiles. When Old Nick rose from the table and pulled on his boots and coat, he turned to them and said, "The simple needs of life are yours, there is plenty of firewood stacked against the side of the house, the rest of the deer is hanging in the barn where the bears can't get it and you have enough food to get you through the worst of winter."

"How can we ever repay you?" Cal called from the doorway as Nick climbed onto the old buckboard.

"Be kind to the next people you meet, keep a peaceful heart, rejoice in the sunshine and be thankful for the rain."

Old Nick always seemed to show up when he was most needed. It seemed he was able to, by his simple presence, stop a fight, heal a heartache, mend a fence, fix a meal, calm, soothe, give hope and share dreams. All this he did with his stories. No one was certain just where he came from. There were some folks in Los Lunas who claimed he was from an old Mexican family that lived down by the river. Folks from Acoma and Laguna insisted he was an Indian, and talked of the stories he told as proof. Up in Albuquerque he was thought to be an Anglo. Some said that he had been a drummer boy in the Civil War and had been wounded in the head. Still others claimed that he was the illegitimate son of a priest from Santa Fe. All this was only speculation. When folks mustered enough courage to ask, Nick would only smile and say, "I come from over the hills, by where the sweet water runs."

This was Old Nick, so kind a man that many looked for the flaws and faults, for the hidden past, the feet of clay. When they couldn't find true flaws, they would make up some. A rumor floated around Grants that he had killed a man down near Las Cruces, another claimed that he had been a gambler and had his hands broken in a fight.

Someone claimed to have known him as a prospector who had stolen a claim. And so the stories multiplied. But most had only good words for this kindly, if bumbling, old man who seemed incapable of holding a real job, yet was always ready to lend a helping hand.

He had been a part of the Territory of New Mexico landscape, one of those truly unique New Mexico characters that make this part of the country so rich. No one could remember him as a young man, only as a wanderer with arthritic hands, a mind that couldn't comprehend business, and a heart bigger than the New Mexico sky. He didn't own a gun, yet walked without fear through the mountains and deserts. He never seemed to have much money, yet was always able to share, provide a meal, or whatever someone needed. He was never seen in a new shirt, yet seemed to be rich beyond all reason in what truly mattered.

His presence brought a sense of peace to all those nearby. He wasn't a doctor or a curandero, yet many had been healed simply by his presence. His calm way with a good story made him a welcome guest at any dinner table, yet he'd never been invited into the homes of the wealthy, the politicians or the powerful people of the territory.

He would tell the stories to sheep herders by the fire at their camps in the warmth of spring, engage in conversation with farmers by the fireplace on a cold winter night, dance the prayers with the Indians and share their wisdom, visit the sick, find a meal for the hungry and provide hope for the desperate. He would show up at the home of a grieving widow and comfort her, guide a wayward youth with gentle words, give strength and courage by his presence to those who felt weak, powerless and fearful.

For years he did this without seeming to age; he was, after all an old man when earliest memories of him were recalled. It was strange, but most of the folks in this region couldn't recall not havin' Old Nick around. It was a comfort that they could count on, the one dependable character in a far from perfect humanity. It was interesting how, as he continued his quiet presence, his peaceful way of living a life by sharing it, others began to do likewise. Neighbors would visit, share the work, share the dinner table and share the stories afterward. The wild west of the dime novels was a myth. The reality was much closer to this quiet, ancient man of peace.

One Christmas Eve he wandered into Albuquerque, to the church of San Felipe de Neri. He stepped inside the doors and removed his hat. He fumbled through his pockets looking for a coin or two for the offering and found three pennies. Those that saw him in the doorway that night said he looked older, thinner. More lines creased his tired face, but that calm smile had never been as broad, the eyes never so full of kindness.

No one knew when he left the church. It had to be sometime during the mass. No one even thought of him all that holy night. They had their parties to go to, wine to drink, songs to sing and prayers to recite. After all, this was the celebration of the birth of the Christ Child, the Prince of Peace, the pathway to salvation.

With the sunrise, the priest came out to dust the snow from the Navidad on the lawn of the church. That's when he saw the old man curled up in the hay behind the carved figure of Joseph. Angry at such a desecration of this holy scene, the priest shook the old man. It was then that he realized that Old Nick had died in the peace of the Holy Family, on the eve of the day set aside to celebrate the birth of the very symbol of peace and love. He was carried into the church and laid at the base of the altar.

Word spread throughout the community and into the surrounding hillsides, to the farms, ranches and pueblos. By noon people were bringing gifts of food and clothing, of handmade tools and works of art. All these gifts were a way of honoring this quiet and peaceful man.

They would be distributed in the next week to the poorest families in the Rio Grande Valley, freely given as a tribute to Old Nick. It became a tradition that continues to this day as hearts are opened; the gifts, often meager, are always shared with love and peace from the heart. Sometimes folks will leave a message to the recipients and sign it, not with their own name, but with "Old Nick" as a tribute to this symbol of living peace.

Tributes were written on scraps of paper, memories of one of the poorest of men who died in the symbol of the most holy of beginnings. He died near the manger where the one called the Prince of Peace had been born.

Many people who visited the church that day brought gifts or wrote a message, but only one seemed to truly understand the meaning in all this. A young girl wrote in her childish scrawl, "Thank you, Jesus, for coming back to us to show us how to behave. Thank you for being with us in the form of this man. Thanks for being Old Nick." She signed her name, than added, "I will pray that you come often to visit people all over the world and teach them how to love each other and live in peace. Just like you did when you were dressed like Old Nick."

In every community we can find Old Nick. In your neighborhood it may be a woman caring for a homeless family, or a teacher spending time with a troubled youth, or an elder telling stories, or a volunteer at a senior meals site, or a chaplain visiting the prisoners, the gardener sharing the produce from his garden, or the lady sharing kind words with the lonely, or the gentle ones who bring smiles to those with fading memories, or the ones giving shelter and food to the stray animals. These are the ones among us who give so freely the gift of hope to all they meet. They too are the light of the season. Perhaps you are one of these, who by your everyday life light the way.

Fallen Angel

Professor Dexter lived in fear. Fear of the loneliness, now that his wife had left him, fear that he would lose his teaching position at UNM, fear that the frequent pain in his chest was the warning of a heart attack. To escape all this fear he hid in a bottle, actually, many of them. He had just emptied another Jim Beam when his blurred eyes saw the flashing neon lights. His vision was so impaired by the alcohol that he couldn't read them, but he was almost certain that he was near the campus. He knew there was a strip joint somewhere nearby and this must be it. He was drawn to the light, like a moth to a candle. But this Christmas Eve, Professor Dexter would not find freedom from his fears in liquid spirits.

The wind was cold and the few snowflakes in the air stung his face. As he came closer to the flashing neon lights, he could see the figure of a woman. Now he was certain that he could get inside and get another drink before he looked for his car in the UNM parking lot behind the Anthro Building, wherever that was. Now, he was afraid he was lost. He had to get another drink, another bottle full of courage. His head hurt. He tried to walk toward the neon lady, but his feet refused to do what he told them.

As he staggered across the parking lot, he saw that this wasn't a neon lady at all. It was an angel surrounded by lights and a sign that said 'SHELTER' and then, in smaller letters, a word that looked like 'kitchen.' There were several benches with an assortment of destitute humanity sitting, or sleeping, on them. Others were leaning against the wall, and several more were stretched out on the asphalt that was now turning white with the snow.

The old lady in nuns' habit with a large wooden cross around her neck came out the door. She smiled broadly and began to speak, striking such a beneficent pose, with a Mona Lisa smile, much like the wooden angel on the wall above her.

Prof. Dexter leaned over to the old man beside him and laughed, "She looks like a damned penguin, doesn't she?" Then he laughed again almost hysterically as he fell backward onto the snoring hulk of a man wrapped in a torn and stained overcoat.

An elderly, bearded man helped him regain his footing and in a harsh whisper scolded him. "She's Sister Evangelista, the nun that runs this soup kitchen. If it wasn't for her, you'd be mighty damn hungry and cold tonight."

She smiled as she walked among the homeless men and women, and the few children who had sought a warm meal, shelter and friendship in the face of this first serious winter weather of the season. She now balanced a large plastic tray in her hands as she spoke. It was cold and they were still preparing the inside of the shelter for a Christmas Eve service.

"Christmas isn't a moment in time, nor is it a merchandising opportunity. Christmas is the universal quest of all humanity for Peace Beyond All Fear."

She paused to offer the chipped and stained coffee mugs filled with steaming hot posole. Then she continued. "The angels spoke 'Fear not, for we bring glad tidings."

But those gathered were now focused on the contents of the coffee mugs. Hunger can be a profound distraction.

As that tray was emptied, an elderly volunteer came out into the cold with another, precariously filled to overflowing with more mugs of steaming posole. Sister Evangelista continued, "That night a baby was born in a stable. He was homeless, in extreme poverty, so vulnerable and helpless. But in reality this babe was the embodiment of the most powerful force on earth, a force that toppled the Roman Empire's military might, a force that is still at work. This is the awesome power of peace, symbolized by the birth of a baby, a message echoed throughout all time to all peoples, all existence, always and forever. This is what this season is about. This is what our faith is about. Peace."

Professor Dexter sat beside the old man, trying very hard to ignore this lady's words. He had given up on churches a long time ago. He was, after all, a social anthropologist. He knew too much about all the different religions. He knew the truth of their mythology, and he knew that the main control religion had over people was the power of fear.

The nun continued again, "Those people 2,000 years ago were living in fear, much as we do today. This fear was used as a way to control them then, as it is today. The fear, born of ignorance was challenged by the Peace born into poverty and homelessness, but born of the ultimate wisdom of all creation."

He stood and started to correct her, "Lady, I wish what you say was true, but . . ." just then a strong gust of wind came around the building and knocked his feet from under him. He would have landed on the pavement had it not been for the couple that grabbed him. The old man seated beside him jumped up and ran to the wall of the building, but he was a moment too late. The wind had torn the wooden angel from its moorings and it came crashing down into the junipers and the brick planter. The wings were shattered.

Father Diaz came out of the door just in time to see the old man holding the angel. Then he saw the shattered wings in the snow. He assumed that this poor homeless soul had somehow torn the angel from the wall. He began, in a most unpriest-like manner, shouting and cursing the old man. Confused, he gently laid the angel in the snow and, shoulders bent, slowly walked off into the night.

Dexter staggered forward to speak for this poor old man who had only tried to help. Sister Evangelista joined him and together they calmed the priest's anger. Everyone was motioned inside as the wind again swirled the increasingly heavy snow through the air. Sister gently lifted the wingless angel in her arms and carried it inside. Prof Dexter knelt and picked up the pieces of shattered wings. Several of the others helped and soon they had all of the bits and pieces spread out on the back table.

Coffee, tea and hot chocolate warmed the thirty-three men, women and children as they dined on more hot posole, tortillas, with biscochitos and gingerbread cookies for dessert. Dr. Dexter had never been inside a homeless shelter before. He was cursing his inebriation. Here was an opportunity to study a deviant culture within a culture, and he was too drunk to organize his thoughts, or even comprehend most of what was happening.

After the third cup of coffee he was able to converse semi-intelligently with the others. He helped as best he could as they cleared the tables and pushed them against the walls to make room for the cots and mattresses. Then he glanced back at the wingless angel standing watch in the corner. His eyes then focused on the broken pieces of the wings. He started crying for that poor broken angel. He sobbed and sobbed. Then with tear-filled eyes, he turned again to the people busy with sheets, blankets and quilts. He saw a lady reading a story to a group of children, but something was wrong. No, maybe not wrong, but different. Each of these people, even the derelicts, drunks and druggies, had wings.

"You're all a flock of angels," he shouted out with slurred speech. But the moment he spoke the wings all fell to the floor. In a softer voice, almost a whisper, he reacted to the fallen and shattered wings now littering the floor. "You're all broken angels."

Suddenly he remembered the old man who had been so frightened by the priest's angry words, even though he was the one who caught the fallen angel and prevented much worse damage. He struggled into his coat and, with unsteady steps, found his way to the door. Sister Evangelista stopped him and put her hand on his shoulder. "You're welcome to spend the night with us. There's room. There's always room here."

But he knew he had to find that old man. It was too cold for him to be out in the wind and the snow. He muttered something about bringing him back and left the momentary warmth, friendship, security and peace that filled that room.

It took some time for his eyes to adjust to the darkness. He walked through the parking lot and over to the hillside and the arroyo below. He thought he could see a dark figure by the Apache plume that lined the edge of the lot. He approached slowly, not wanting to startle the figure that didn't seem to be moving. As he reached the old man, he again felt fear grabbing him by the throat, but this time it was concern for someone else. It was the kind of fear that gave him the courage to try to awaken the figure slumped against the shrubs. His face felt cold, but he opened his eyes and tried to smile. Professor Dexter removed his coat and wrapped it around the old man. The combination of cold and compassion sobered the professor, and gave him strength he didn't know he possessed. He helped the old man up, and helped him back to the shelter.

After the old man was warmed with hot tea and the last of the posole, he tried again to apologize and explain that he was trying to rescue the falling angel, "But I failed. Just like I failed at everything else I ever tried."

Dr. Dexter had walked back to the kitchen to get himself another cup of coffee. He looked out on the now thirty-four people, observing them with almost sober eyes. Such diversity this group exhibited. A thought struck him as he watched this rag tag assemblage of Anglos,

34

Hispanics, Native Americans, Afro-Americans and Asian-Americans. These people are all parents, children, aunts, uncles, cousins, nieces and nephews, but they weren't with those families.

He turned to Sister Evangelista and started to put into words the revelation that had just come to him, "These people all have known crushing poverty, physical and mental illness, the ravages of drugs, alcohol, crime, and the despair of profound loss, loss of respect and acceptance, loss of self-respect, loss of hope. They're all living in fear. They live at the bottom of this city's culture, but they also support each other. They have survived through cooperation rather than competition."

She smiled at his words, but continued her work, the work of compassion, of providing a moment of respite for lives so dominated by hopelessness.

He studied these people again as they began to relax in the warmth of this nun's smile, and the sense of the peace that dwelt in this place. It was several moments before he realized again that there were wings glowing on these people.

He turned his attention to the old man now engaged in conversation with Sister Evangelista. He too had wings. He carried his coffee mug over to their table. As he was about to pull one of the folding chairs over and sit down, the old man stood on shaky legs and extended his hand, "Thanks mister. My name's Gabriel. I'm afraid I would have been a goner if you hadn't come along."

"He went out in the cold and the snow looking for you" Sister Evangelista commented as she patted Dr. Dexter on the back. "He's the one who told us about you trying to save our angel."

Gabriel looked over at the bits and pieces of the wings spread out on the table. "I'm afraid that we're never going to put that back together."

Dr. Dexter leaned forward, elbows on the table, looking deep into the old man's eyes. "Nothing to be afraid of friend," he said. "All we need are some extra hands and a bottle of glue." He leaned back in his chair and smiled, "At the Maxwell Museum we glue 1000 year old pots back together. Come on. Let's see what we can do."

Within minutes, Gabriel and the professor were sorting out the pieces. Soon several others joined them, and in a few more minutes almost everyone was gathered around the table. Homer started playing an old John Denver song, "Falling Leaves," a hymn about refugees and the homeless that Denver had written back in 1987. Soon everyone was singing Christmas carols, in several languages, sometimes several different songs were being sung at the same time. It was way past the normal bedtime for these folks, but everyone sensed that something special was happening.

Gradually, piece after piece was fitted together, like a three dimensional jigsaw puzzle. Finally, long past midnight, the wings had been restored to their former faded weathered grandeur. But it was Gabriel who pointed out something most strange. There were still pieces of the broken wings left. They carried the reconstructed wings into the bright light and examined them from every angle. There were no pieces missing. These wings were whole.

35

Sister Evangelista held one of these extra pieces in her hand. "I think I have an idea, she said as she picked up a paring knife and began whittling and carving. Within minutes she held up her mini-sculpture. It was a pair of tiny angel's wings. She took Gabriel's frail and arthritic hand, and carefully opened it. She placed the wings in his palm. "There. I think you have earned your wings," she said with a smile.

Dexter and several of the others began whittling the bits that were left. But is seemed that there were still more pieces on the table. By the time the first rays of the morning sun were leaving glittering tracks across the pure white snow, everyone in the shelter had a pair of angel wings, a reminder to seek the higher ground and share the peace they had found.

Still, there were pieces of wood left. Now those who had slept took over the knives and scraps of an angel's wings. By the time the breakfast meal was over, they had more than a hundred more angel's wings spread out on the tables. There was one small piece left. Gabriel was exhausted, but he picked it up and began to carve. He was bent over, working slowly but meticulously. Finally, he sat back and handed his creation to Dexter. It was a dove with its wings folded and its head bent in prayer. "This is for you, my friend," He said. "Carry this with you and let it remind you of the peace that the dove carries for us all, The Peace Beyond All Fear."

Peace Beyond All Fear is the title of a collection of short stories that was written as a tribute to the vision and work of John Denver. This was the title story and was inspired by a song John Denver, born Henry John Deutchendorf in Roswell, NM on December 31, 1943, wrote about the refugees and the homeless of the world. That song is Falling Leaves. While this is sometimes viewed as a Christmas hymn, it is a song for all seasons and all ages. The author hopes you will find the song on YouTube or a CD and listen to this beautiful and powerful message as a part of your celebration of this season.

The White Donkey

The desert is a harsh land with little water. A place where survival is often all one can hope for. Yet there is a comfort to be found in the solitude, the simple beauty, blue skies, bright sun and the star filled nights. In the desert one can find the simple purity and raw essence of life, the truth of who we are and where we fit into the beauty of all creation.

It has been the custom as long as the people of the desert have herded the goats and sheep and cattle, that the lowly donkey is the most dependable pack animal. This creature has been more than simply the beast of burden. The donkey, or burro, has for untold centuries been a companion to these desert travelers. Donkeys are strong even though they are small, and loyal to the point of being a dependable friend for those lonely and alone. They have accompanied us on great adventures, shared in our discoveries and our losses.

In a time that seems long ago, but is really only a moment, less than a line on the pages of humanity's story, there was, in this desert place, a trader, and an old, grey-haired donkey loaded with bags and chests of goods. So great was the burden that one could scarcely see the poor beast beneath. It was as they neared a crudely dug well at the side of the trail that the donkey stumbled under the weight and fell to its knees.

It was at the very moment the trader was plying his whip, struggling to get this ancient beast to his feet, that he spied a younger, much stronger, donkey standing off to the side seeking scant shade in the rocks beside the well. He took his rope and, with soothing sounds and calming gestures, approached this find. All the while, he was looking around for the possible owner of such a fine beast of burden.

The rope was secure around the neck of this newfound treasure and water was shared with it. Then, his new possession secured by the rope to a thorn tree, he returned to the sorry old donkey still lying by the side of the road. He untied the bags, bundles, boxes and chests and kicked the old creature in the ribs twice, cursing all the while.

Without the heavy load, the poor old creature was able to regain its footing and stood on the road for a few minutes, then began to slowly walk toward the well for a drink.

"Away, you useless animal." He shouted and struck it with the whip several times. "Out of my sight."

The poor old donkey was confused but trotted off, lest he be struck again. The trader gave the new donkey a handful of grain and made camp for the night. The old donkey circled the well several times longing for a drink, but afraid of the trader and the whip.

With the rising sun the new donkey was loaded with the goods and their journey continued. The ancient beast, so grey he looked white in the bright desert sun, stood by the well, but was unable to reach the water below.

Finally, it was about evening, the sun was casting bright red and gold streaks across the western sky. In the distance a man and his young wife knelt in prayer. Their journey had been long and hard. She was barely more than a child, yet she was with child herself. The man lifted his eyes to the setting sun and saw, in the golden glow of a sunbeam, a brilliant white donkey standing beside a well. Their thirst had been great and the walk so difficult for his wife. His first thought was that perhaps he could buy this beast so that his wife could ride the rest of their journey. Then he realized that a beast such as this would cost far more than he could pay. Still there was a well, and their thirst could at least be quenched.

Down the hillside they came, ever so slowly in the sand and stones that bruised their feet. She pointed out as they neared the well that there was no one around who could possibly be the donkey's owner. But as they came closer, what had seemed a magnificent white donkey proved to be nothing more than an aging, sway-backed beast, probably useless as a pack animal. Most likely it had been abandoned, left for the wolves. He pulled a bucket of water from the well and gave the first drink to his wife, had a drink himself, then sat the bucket for the donkey to satisfy its thirst. They shared what bread they had left with the aged beast.

The night was spent at the well, then, in the dawning light the donkey again appeared to be glowing white in the bright rays of the morning sun. It came close to them, looking much stronger. It was obviously a gift from a loving and compassionate Creator. A God that cared so much for even the beasts of burden that He gave them the strength to repay the gifts of kindness; gave the gift of an opportunity to carry a pregnant girl home to the Laguna pueblo for Christmas after a long and difficult journey to receive the blessing of her husband's family in Taos. The burro spoke a prayer of thanks to the Great Mystery as the mother- to-be was helped onto his back for the rest of their journey.

Such was the life in the high desert of Nuevo Mexico in the 1700's.

Home for Christmas

This is a story told years ago. As with most good stories shared over hot coffee on a cold night, it has been told in a variety of ways. While it's a story of hope in difficult times, it's also a story of simple and profound faith. In the bleak and hopeless days of the Great Depression, families were forced from their homes. Sometimes the desperation of poverty, hunger and the fear of what tomorrow may bring, was answered by simple acts of kindness. And that continues in today's world as well. Within each of us is the opportunity to be the answer to someone else's prayers. Hope may be found in the distant lights seen through a snowstorm. Each of us can be the light, provide the refuge from the storm, serve the warm meal on a cold night, share the kind words and open hearts that define the season for all people.

"I'm cold, and my feet are all wet." Lisa sobbed and tugged at Daddy's flannel jacket. She was too tired to avoid the puddle of slushy snow and almost freezing water.

As he reached down to take her in his arms, Ricardo felt the pain his daughter felt. His feet were cold for her. His legs ached from the walking she had done this day. And he felt her fear and confusion in his heart. In quiet prayer he asked God to let him have her suffering, and the pain and hopelessness of his wife Rosa as well.

"Oh God," he whispered to the sky, "Please give me their suffering. It is my fault they have no warm fire, new clothes, laughter and friends on Christmas Eve, not even a dry shelter from the storm." He shifted her weight to his other arm, "Please, Mother of God, let me have their pain and misery. Please, put this burden on my shoulders."

He prayed in silence, but Rosa read the words in his tears. She took his hand in hers and searched for some comforting words, but the effort became another spasm of coughing. This only increased his sense of guilt and failure.

It had been a dismal day with first snow then rain, not a real rain, but one of those fine mists that chills you to the bone. His mother called this pneumonia weather. It was only a few years ago that she had been working in such a rain back at his childhood home in Portales, that first sent her to bed, then, less than two weeks later, to her grave. His fists were clenched white knuckle tight with a pain somewhere between fear and despair. He could not let this happen to Rosa and little Lisa. He looked skyward as if this would somehow force God to take notice, hear him and respond.

The wind caught his hat and it took a swift grab to catch it. This made Lisa laugh. One of the gifts of childhood is the ability to live in the moment and free oneself to be captivated. As he placed his hat on Lisa's head, causing more laughter, Rosa pointed down the hill, shouting, "Look! Look!"

Ricardo at first thought she was calling their attention to the great heavy snowflakes that were replacing the rain as this gray day was becoming a cold night. Then he too saw the dim and distant lights down in the valley far ahead. In this glow was the glimmer of hope they could cling to. Perhaps there would be food and shelter, another human voice.

When he lost his job in El Paso, he had written a letter to his brother Ramon in Santa Cruz, New Mexico. It was almost two months later when he finally received a note back, and it wasn't reassuring. Ramon had written that there was no work there either, but, of course, there was room in his house if they needed a place to stay. That was one of the strengths of the Sanchez family. They would always be there to take care of each other.

Ricardo had worked for five years as a farm laborer for Dwayne Gribbs, doing all the things that had to be done to produce the tomatoes and fruit for the cannery. The Gribbs Farms label meant something and he was proud to be a part of it. That label claimed the highest prices; that was until the market collapsed in '29. Two years later a bank failure forced the Gribbs family to sell out. Now Ricardo was unemployed.

He recovered from the shock of being jobless and began searching for work with hopefulness. "Maybe this is really an opportunity. Maybe," he told Rosa, "This will force me to find a job that pays real money. Soon, maybe, we will be able to make a down payment on a farm of our own."

Rosa smiled at his optimism, but deep inside she knew there was little chance of her husband finding work in the middle of this depression. She was scared, but she held it all inside until the transmission fell out of their old Chevy truck on the way to visit her family in Amarillo. Now there was no way to get to work, even if he could find a job.

"Thank God," she wept on his shoulder, "Thank God I still have my job."

Rosa was a waitress at the Mexicali Café, but, when the depression hit, it seemed that all the restaurants and lunch counters were either closing or laying off. When Miguel, the owner, called her into the back room and handed her the envelope with $50 in it, she just stared at him. He was an old man, and this was so difficult for him. He motioned for her to be seated and explained that business was dead, that he was going to have to close the doors, that today was her last day of work. She sat dumbfounded, trying to understand what this meant. Finally, she gave him a hug, thanked him, and started to cry. She cried all the way home, a walk of almost a mile. She was twenty four years old and had been a waitress there since she was fifteen. She knew nothing else.

Ricardo tried to comfort her long into the night, but they knew that with both of them unemployed, what little they had saved in the Jar of Dreams would never be used to buy a farm of their own, and would only pay the rent for a few months. There was also Lisa, three years old and depending on them to take care of her.

The eviction notice came two days before the letter from Ramon. They packed what they could into bundles they could carry and, with most of their remaining money, bought bus tickets to Santa Cruz. They were clinging to the hope that with family they might all survive this great depression.

Santa Cruz was a small town, so the first person they met listened patiently as they briefly told their story and asked if she knew where they could find Ramon's house. She motioned for them to be seated on the bench by the well. With tears in her eyes, she explained, "I am so sorry. A great tragedy has fallen on Ramon and his family." She took Rosa's hand in hers before continuing, "Their house has burned to the ground."

The shock of this news hit Ricardo and Rosa hard. Tears flowed as the old lady led them to her house for some coffee and tamales. She doubted that they were still there, but had no idea where Ramon, his wife and two children would have gone. "I remember him telling me he had a brother down in El Paso." She said as they asked for directions to the remains of the house. "If you must see what's left, just follow the dirt road out of town to the north about five miles. It will be the second lane on the left. The family escaped the fire without injuries, thank heavens. I think they may still be staying in the barn."

Words could not describe the despair that hit them as they rounded the bend in the lane and the burned out remains of what had housed their last hope came into view. The fire had been perhaps two weeks ago, but the smell of burnt wood and roofing still hung in the air. It was the stench of hope destroyed and the ashes of dreams that assailed their senses. Lisa began to sob. There were no fresh tracks in the snow around the small barn. The damp chill in the air made them shiver, but it was also the coldness of despair for themselves and concern for their family. They entered the shelter of the old barn and spent the night. The next morning they were on the road again, now wandering with little hope of finding Ramon and his family. Ricardo wasn't familiar with the area. As the day progressed and the breezes became cold winter winds, they were driven forward by fear, but now they had no destination. They wandered from village to town, spent one night in an abandoned miner's shack, another sharing the campfire of a sheepherder who had seen Ramon a few days before, who told them, "He mentioned something about you folks being down on your luck and needing to find a way to help." He shrugged his shoulders, but didn't reply.

Usually, they found shelter and sympathetic assistance in the small towns that dotted the hillsides like jewels; sympathy, but no news of Ramon and his family, and no jobs. Occasionally there was a church and a modest meal from a kindly priest or nun. The last two nights had been spent along the side of the road. These hills were without even a small farm.

Christmas Eve came without hope, without peace in their hearts. That was until Rosa saw the distant lights through the twilight snow. It was with renewed vigor that this shivering and hungry trio set their steps toward the light, toward the faint glimmer of hope. The snow storm was increasing in intensity now. They were almost running as they neared the lights. These were farilitos, the candles that illuminated the pathway of stars leading the way to the Christ Child.

41

This was a glorious display and all three were in awe as they followed the path to the elaborate door of a grande hacienda. There was a juniper spray on the door to welcome guests and chile ristras and strings of corn and garlics spoke of comfort and plenty to be found inside.

"I don't think such people will welcome vagrants like us," Ricardo whispered as Rosa hesitantly knocked on the massive carved door.

Ricardo pushed Lisa to the front, whispering, "Who can deny a child like this on Christmas Eve?"

While they waited for someone to open the door, they straightened their clothes and tried to look as presentable as possible. Finally, the door opened and the light from within was almost blinding. The warmth of a fireplace hit them in the face and the delightful scent of pinon burning in the fireplace teased their senses. There were also wonderful aromas from the kitchen, chiles, roast, fresh bread and apple empanadas.

The rather slender man with the neatly trimmed salt and pepper beard stood in the doorway for a moment studying the guests shivering on the portico. Then he smiled and turned his head, "Mary, come here. We have guests."

He knelt down and took Lisa's hand in his, "Hello! My name is Joe, and what might your name be?" As she shyly responded, he turned his attention to Ricardo and Rosa. "It's a nasty night to be out roaming about. This being Christmas Eve, won't you join us for some dinner and a warm fire?"

There was a large deep green juniper in the corner. Tiny ears of corn, cornhusk dolls, chile peppers, clay figures of animals and saints, brightly painted gourds and gilded walnuts adorned the tree. On a small wooden table was a creche with clay figures of the Nativity. On the floor before the fireplace was a large Navajo rug. That's where Lisa and Rosa sat to warm themselves before the flames. Mary left the room, but returned moments later with a rag doll. Lisa thanked her profusely and soon fell asleep to the comforting sound of the snapping pinon fire.

Joe called them to the table for a meal that was like a feast to them. "We don't get much company up here in the mountains, so we really enjoy folks when they do come around." He passed the fresh bread, warm from the oven, and continued, "You see, our son has grown to be a man and he works with his Father." He offered no explanation to satisfy the questioned looks from Rosa and Ricardo.

During the course of the meal Ricardo told their story, and about how they were now searching for Ramon and his wife and children.

After supper and a glass of wine, they went back into the kiva shaped living room and Joe pulled some wrapped packages from beneath the tree. He handed Rosa a heavy box and a lumpy, irregular shaped package wrapped in calico cloth. She was delighted with the warm woolen poncho, but puzzled by the pottery mixing bowl filled with dough.

Mary laughed, "That's sourdough starter. It'll last a lifetime if you keep it fed and share it with friends and strangers alike."

42

Ricardo opened the first of his packages and wept over the kindness of such people who would give strangers warm clothing and other gifts. The second package was very heavy and awkwardly shaped. He pulled back the burlap bag that served as the gift wrap to reveal a shovel head, hoe head and an axe without handles.

"A good farmer always wants to craft his own tool handles," Joe explained.

Lisa was overwhelmed by the new fleece lined boots, leather mittens, a coloring book and a box of crayons. There was one more small box that Mary told them they could open together. When Lisa untied the bow and pulled back the cloth that served as the wrapping, a most precious gift was revealed. It was a box filled to the top with packets of seeds; corn, squash, beans, tomato seeds, chile seeds and many more.

While Ricardo, Rosa and Lisa spread the packets out on the floor, Mary explained, "These are for the garden you will plant together in the spring. The garden is a promise from God that the sun will shine, that the rain will fall and that body and soul will be sustained."

They visited long into the night. Lisa fell asleep in Rosa's arms, and Ricardo began to yawn. Joe and Mary led them into a guest room and lit a fire in the fireplace for them. Then they bid the tired family good night and departed.

They thanked God profusely as they knelt beside the bed. Then as they pulled the warm quilt over Lisa and climbed into bed themselves, they began to feel guilty. They had nothing to give in return for the generosity they had received. They were ashamed and vowed to leave very early in the morning before their benefactors were awake.

They took the clothes because they needed the warmth, but left the tools, mixing bowl and seeds behind, because they didn't want to appear greedy. They walked north until dawn before they paused to rest.

"OH! Madre Dios!" Rosa exclaimed, "We didn't even leave them a note of thanks." Rosa suggested that they make some more ornaments for the juniper tree. While mother and daughter gathered pine cones, seed pods and twigs, Ricardo gathered a large bundle of firewood. So large was this bundle that Rosa had to help tie it and secure the straps that would hold it on his back. Then, they set out to, in this small way, repay the kindness.

As they approached the town in the daylight, they could see that it was a deserted ghost of a town, devoid of a living soul. They looked up and down the street, empty, except for snow-covered tumbleweed. They could find nothing that resembled the grand hacienda where they had spent the night. At the end of the street was an old abandoned adobe mission. Bewildered, they almost fearfully entered the crumbling church to pray. As they knelt, he saw the mixing bowl, the tools and the seeds against what was once a finely carved altar.

When he opened his eyes again from prayer Lisa shouted, "Look, look at the light!"

Streaming in the window was a sunbeam illuminating the altar and the gifts they had been given the night before.

After more prayers of thanks they set about cleaning the abandoned structure. It was late in the afternoon when they heard voices. Ricardo rushed to the door to greet his brother, his wife and their children.

In the weeks that followed, these two families clean and repaired several of the buildings. Soon others, homeless and hopeless, found their way to this ghost town. All were welcomed and a new community was created from this forgotten village. Because no one knew what this place had once been called, they christened the reborn Pueblo de la Esperanza, Village of Hope. And in the spring they all planted the seeds, shared the labor and the harvest

This is the way the story was told to us.

Lighting the Way

Alberto is an old man and the children still come with their candles, an old man who lives alone in the shack down the hill and across the road from the Iglesia de Santa Clara de Assisi. It's a tiny chapel in serious need of repairs, with seating for about three dozen souls. At one time it was a rare Sunday when more than half of the seats were filled, but today Sunday morning mass draws overflow crowds.

It was served by a priest slightly older than Alberto himself. The ancient Father Griego continues to make the trek to this once forgotten community twice a month. Today tourists are more plentiful visitors to this church than the faithful. They flock to this iglesia for one reason only, the walls are lined with santos, bultos and retablos, all done by the skilled hands of a master santero, a carver of the saints. That is Alberto, famous far beyond this village, far beyond the borders of New Mexico.

He has always been uncomfortable with the endless visits, requests for photographs and autographs. He is most troubled by those waving money at him, wanting to buy his art. He has not sold a single one of the santos he has made since that day his wife and only son died in the flood so many years ago.

He continues to blame himself for their death. He had spent his youth in the bars and at the cockfights and gaming places. He also spent a good deal of time in the local jail.

Without money to buy food, Nolina and Roberto had been in the arroyo gathering greens for the evening meal and looking for arrowheads and pottery shards to sell. The storm came suddenly and the wall of water caught them as they tried to climb the banks. Alberto was sleeping off a three day drunk and never even heard the thunder.

God had punished him for his sins of neglect and revelry. To atone, he set about to become a carver of santos. He lacked the grand tools of the professionals in Santa Fe, all he had to work with were ancient chisels and hand-me-down hand mallets, some he even rescued from the dump. He had lived a life of incredible poverty, sadness and guilt until that eventful Christmas.

But let's go back to the beginning of the story of this legendary santero who still lives in a shack without electricity, a telephone or running water.

It was the day he lost his family that he took down the gun from the mantle and gathered every bit of liquor, every bottle he had hidden around the house. These he took out into the yard, lined them up along the fence and shot every last one of them. Then he pointed the gun at his head and uttered a prayer. He begged God to welcome the souls of Nolina and little Roberto. He closed his eyes and pulled the trigger. There was a click, nothing more. He opened his eyes just in time to see a nun carrying a large santo into the church across the road.

God had spared him, and he was convinced that his punishment was to live, live with the guilt, never escaping the sorrow, and the shame. After the funerals, on the way back from the little cemetery, the young priest walked with Alberto to the house. Sitting at the table Father Griego heard the story of the gun that wouldn't work and the nun at the church. "This is a message to you from our Holy Father in Heaven." The priest spoke as he crossed himself. "You are to atone for your drinking by carving a santo for our modest chapel."

"But, but, I have no skill in carving. I am not an artist."

"God will use your hands. God is the artist." The priest countered, "It is God's will. This is obvious because of your vision."

"I have seen no vision. At least none that didn't come from a bottle." Alberto argued.

"Didn't you tell me just minutes ago about seeing the nun carrying a santo into the chapel?"

"Yes, but that wasn't a vision," he countered.

"My friend, we have no nun serving this house of worship. Nor do we have a single santo here." He placed his hand on Alberto's shoulder. "This was a message from God. This is what you are to do. You must create a santo for la Iglesia de Santa Clara de Assisi." He prayed for the mourning Alberto before departing for other duties elsewhere.

Alberto, with the approaching darkness of evening, went to the wood pile to gather enough fuel to cook dinner and keep the fire going for the night. There was one piece of cedar, about two feet long with a branch at the side. The bark was peeling from it and gave the appearance of a cloak. Alberto was certain that he could see a face within the wood, and an arm outstretched. As he held this piece of firewood before him, he could see a candle in that outstretched hand.

He built a fire and put the coffee pot on the stove. Tears flowed down his cheeks and one by one dripped onto the piece of wood that he held in his lap. He later insisted that it was these tears that showed him where to apply the blade of his old dull hunting knife. He spent the night drinking coffee, feeding the fire in the stove and whittling away with the oversized and awkward knife.

With the first rays of the morning sun, a figure was emerging from the wood. It was the figure of a young woman, head lifted in hope and expectation. The carving was crude, but proportion was good, and there was that outstretched arm. The bright rays of the rising sun came through the window and illuminated that arm and what would soon become a hand. Alberto later told everyone that he could see the candle in her hand, and the smile on her face, a face that

46

hadn't been carved yet. He then knew that this was Santa Clara de Assisi, patron saint of the light leading the way.

He worked through the morning; then finally, exhausted, he fell asleep at the table. The knife fell to the floor. When he awakened hours later, he studied the wooden figure before him. It was obvious that he had done as much as he could with that sorry excuse for a knife. He walked to the neighbor's and asked the lady, Alisandra Sanchez if he could borrow one of her late husband's carpentry chisels. Alisandra didn't like this man, didn't trust him and his drinking, but she felt sorry for him because of the loss of his family. She had been at the funeral yesterday, and she meant to take some food over to him, but feared that he would be sleeping off the effects of the whiskey that he seemed to view as his best friend.

Her earliest childhood had taught her to be cautious of drunks, to stay out of their way, because they could be violent, vulgar and abusive. Her husband had been a carpenter of limited skill, but a good man and a hard worker. In fact some said that he was addicted to work and it was agreed by all that he had worked himself to death. He had died of a heart attack two years ago. Alisandra hadn't even opened the door to his shop since the day she came home from the funeral.

She took the padlock key from the peg by the door and without a word of condolence led the way to the shop. She was shaking so violently by the time they reached the door that she was forced to give him the key. With steady fingers, with hands that now possessed purpose, he worked the lock and opened the door.

She had vowed that she was never again going to enter this shack. Several months after the funeral she gathered the can of lamp oil and matches with the intension of burning it to the ground, but something held her back. She returned to the house and wept for hours, tears of grief, tears of healing.

Yet, now she followed Alberto into the dark structure and led the way to the tool rack above the heavy wooden workbench. There still lingered the comforting smell of wood and sawdust. The late afternoon light streamed through the window, illuminating the tool rack, and, on the bench, an almost completed jewelry box, an unfinished gift for her. A gift she didn't know existed until this moment.

For the first time she was comfortable in this little shop. For the first time she was able to accept her husband's absence. She looked at Alberto with mixture of sympathy and relief, "Take whatever tools you need," she picked up the jewelry box and clutched it to her breast. "Keep the key and use any of the wood, any of the tools, in fact, you are welcome to use this shop if you wish to do your work with wood."

He carefully selected two chisels, the smallest of the three wooden mallets and a well worn sanding stone. Then he turned to the light streaming in the window, crossed himself and muttered a prayer. He returned to his two room house and opened a can of beans for his first meal since the funeral. Sleep came fitfully through the long night and he awoke with the first rays of sunshine. As soon as the fire was started in the stove the coffee was set to brew. It was when he turned from the stove that he noticed the light shining on the half completed santo.

He moved the kitchen table over to the window and placed the chair so that he could work in the light. There he studied the work before him, unsure what to do next, insecure in this new role of santero. Finally, after the second cup of coffee, he took chisel in hand and pressed it to the wood. He worked without stopping all morning, first with one chisel, then with the other, sometimes drawing the blade toward him, sometimes tapping gently with the mallet. He was possessed by a skill and power beyond himself. He was driven with a sense of purpose like he had never known before. Later he insisted that his hands had been guided by a power greater than his.

The table was ideally placed so that the afternoon sun struck it from the window across the room. When that was gone, he lit the oil lamp and continued late into the night. He twice stopped to sharpen the chisels. The form was distinct, but far from complete when he finally fell asleep at the table well after midnight.

He labored for more than a week with this santo. Twice he visited the workshop and borrowed more tools, sanding stones, a carving knife and a saw. He wasn't pleased with the eyes, they seemed uneven, the whole piece of statuary leaned, even after using the saw twice to improve the base, it still seemed to lean.

He stood and seized the mallet in his hand, ready to smash the wooden figure lying on the table. But, he couldn't do it. Instead he threw the mallet with all the force he could muster against the wall.

He left the house and walked the half mile to Diablo's Bar & Grill. The regular afternoon crowd of three or four old men was at the bar reliving their yesterdays while fearing their tomorrows. Alberto was welcomed with words of sympathy and offers of beers all around.

He tried to tell these men about the santo but they were more concerned with rehashing the demise of Nolina and Roberto. This was a subject he didn't want to deal with, couldn't deal with. So he left the beer untouched and walked out. This was the last time in over half a century that he has set foot in a bar. He went to the grocery and tried to get a bag of flour and some beans, but was told that his bill was already too high. He went to the farm where he worked part time when he was sober, but there would be no work for several weeks, but Ernie Sanchez did give him some eggs, a side of bacon and a bag of potatoes.

In the dusk he walked the dirt road home. The tears stung his eyes on this long walk. With the darkness came the damp cold of spring. He shivered from the chill and the sorrow, but mostly from his loneliness.

He opened the door to his humble home and lit the oil lamp. There standing on the table as straight and tall as could be, was the wooden image that he had devoted so much time to. While he had focused on the unevenness of the eyes earlier in the day, now he was drawn to the gentle smile of compassion on her face.

He started a fire, fried himself some potatoes and bacon and made a pot of coffee. As he ate this simple meal, he talked with the wooden figure. He told her of the grief, guilt and loneliness that he felt. The sanding stones were plied with a gentle hand, with patience and a commitment unlike anything he had ever known before.

He sanded, smoothed, polished and shined the wooden lady. With each passing hour his hands became steadier, his mind more confident and his soul more comforted. Morning sun found him still sitting at the table, rubbing the lines of her robe with a piece of old denim jeans. The face seemed to glow, the smile was beautiful, but the eyes were still wrong. Then the voice spoke in his mind, "Open her eyes so that she can see the light."

It took only minutes with the smallest chisel to carve the eyes open. In the process he was able to make them even. He carved them looking heavenward. Combined with the smile, this was a most beautiful santo. He smiled himself as he viewed the work. It was while he was giving a prayer of thanks for the guidance of his hands that he heard the bells ringing from the church across the road.

Alberto went to the stove and put on a pot of water to wash and shave. He was going to church today and he would take the santo with him.

He was closing the door when he looked at the wooden saint's outstretched arm and the empty hand. He went back inside and rummaged through the drawer until he found the stump of a candle. It was less than a minute before the candle was trimmed to fit into the hand of the lady of light, Santa Clara de Assisi. The figure was wrapped in an old sheet, then he set his feet toward the church.

Part two

Father Griego was pleased to see Alberto, but when he unwrapped the figure he fell to his knees. He proclaimed this a miracle and placed the figure in front of the altar so that all could see her. As the services began, the light streamed through the window and the figure glowed. Alberto stepped forward and lit the candle.

It was unfortunate that there were only twelve faithful gathered that Sunday morning because the sermon was as inspired work of art, as was the santo of this church's patron saint.

It seemed to those who had shared this small community with him that this young man in his late thirties had aged greatly in the past weeks. It was strange to watch his face as the faithful complimented him on his artistry and thanked him for his gift to the church. Each kind word brought pain, each handshake brought waves of guilt and renewed grief. This was done for penance, not praise. Why didn't they understand? His family was dead because he had failed to provide for them. And all they could talk about was the smile on this Lady of Light.

Finally, sadder than ever, he walked alone to his house. The clouds were building for a spring storm. It was a dark day for his eyes and for his soul. He stopped at the wood pile and gathered enough wood to keep the old stove fueled through the rest of the day and the inevitable night.

The sorrow became despair as he sat at the table, empty now that the focus of his existence for the past two weeks was holding a place of honor in the empty church. He looked out the window at the adobe structure, painted white, simple in line, the tin roof rusting, but above all empty, as empty as his life was again.

He whispered to the Lady of Light, "Are you as lonely as I? Are you filled with sadness because you are the only santo in that church?"

He started the fire in the stove and put on some hot water for some tea, cota tea made from a wild plant that Nolina had gathered last year. The coffee was gone, as was the money, as was the will to live. The storm clouds covered the valley now, the rain spattered the window and the thunder rumbled and echoed again and again. It was so dark, yet he couldn't light the lamp in the middle of the day, that would waste the oil, and there was precious little left.

He placed some kindling in the fireplace and reached up on the mantle for the matches. He saw the gun hanging there; thought of the earlier failure to end his miserable existence, and took it from the peg. He checked the chamber and sat in the chair beside the empty table, empty except for the wood chips and sanding dust, all that remained of his labor. He had just cocked the hammer when the lightning flashed and the thunder rocked the house. The lightning was brighter that the midday sun and it illuminated the entire room.

It seemed to focus on several pieces of the cedar firewood that he had intended for the fireplace. The violence of the thunder had caused them to slide from the hearth. The two smaller ones were irregular, bent by nature and broken by his hands as he had prepared them for the fire. They formed an off angle cross. The others, one larger, almost too big for the fireplace, and two others had slid down and now he could see plainly that this was a figure, free from the cross with arms stretched toward heaven.

God had taken the gun from his hands a second time and given him another task to perform, another act of penance. For this he lit the lamp and began to peel the bark from the broken cross. It was a simple task and by early morning he was using the smaller carving knife to etch the lines that would define the broken cross. It was then that he missed the wood and pierced the palm of his hand with the sharp knife. It was a small wound and only a few drops of blood fell onto the wood.

At first he was angry with himself for ruining this work, but then he realized that his blood would be as much a part of it as the wood itself. The first rays of the rising sun at that moment shined through the window onto these pieces of wood. In the glow of that light he cut them to fit and secured these two sticks together with a single nail. The cross was broken and bloody as it lay in the glow of the newly risen sun.

Alberto, exhausted, found his way to the unmade bed and slept until the knock on the door late in the afternoon. It was two ladies from the village. They brought two baskets of food: coffee, tortillas and tamales. While he tried to understand what was happening, they cleaned the

50

outer room, put on coffee and heated the tamales in the pot, then swept the wood shavings and dust from the table and the floor. They spent a long time discussing the broken cross on the table, repeatedly pointing to the bloodstains and the broken arms of the cross itself. These sticks had been crudely squared and had the appearance of being roughhewn with an ax.

Finally, the older one turned to him, "Is this also for the church?"

As he nodded in affirmation, the other exclaimed, "Our village is blessed with a santero. Who would have ever though it would be our own drunken Alberto."

The santo itself was a far more difficult task. The chisels were dull. His hands ached and he became weaker and weaker because he was so involved in the carving that he was forgetting to eat. In fact, there were days when he consumed only the cota tea and a corn tortilla. He borrowed a grinding wheel from the carpenter's widow. She insisted that he take the rest of the chisels with him.

For weeks he lived with the conviction that when he finished this santo his soul would be set free. He prayed daily that he would die.

The pilgrimage to the chapel on Ash Wednesday was almost more effort than he could muster. After heating the water to bathe and shave he fell across the bed and slept until the bells called the faithful and devout of the village. He quickly cleansed his body, shaved and put on the cleanest shirt, the one with only a few stains on it.

He walked past the figure on the table, surrounded by wood chips and shavings. It looked at him with incredibly sad eyes, its arms stretching up to him. It seemed to be pleading with him to pick it up and carry it with him to its future home.

Alberto paused, trying to understand what was wrong with this figure. Why was this santo such a difficult project? Perhaps it was true. He wasn't a santero. He couldn't really carve holy figures from scraps of wood. He was nothing more than a hopeless reprobate with no reason to live, no reason for God to let him live, but to punish him for failing his family. The guilt again overwhelmed him, but the bell, sonorous and mournful, rang again, called to him one more time. He walked with slow steps to the doorway of the chapel.

Father Griego took his hand and led him inside. He was about to kneel, but instead he fell over. There was silence throughout the small assemblage.

Frieda Montero, the local curendara, finally approached with a handful of dried yerba buena leaves. She called for water and in less than a minute Alberto was revived. They helped him to the bench, and the service commenced. The ashes marked his forehead and the backs of his hands. He had asked for a special blessing for these hands, that they might be skillful in the completion of his second carving of atonement.

The children, Josephina and her brother, Juan, knocked on the door as the sun was setting over the hills to the west. They were the oldest children of perhaps the only people in the valley poorer than Alberto himself. Together they carried a basket of food into the first room and sat it by the wood stove. There was a bag of coffee, hot steaming tamales, red chile stew and fried potatoes with onions. The children explained as they set the table for him that Father Griego feared he wasn't eating enough, so Mama wanted to share some of their dinner with him.

While Josephina placed the food on the table, Juan brushed away the wood chips and lit candles. They illuminated the figure and both of the children were awed with the detail of the robe, the arms and the hands. Juan crossed himself and whispered, "Es Jesu, aqui es Jesu Cristo!"

She studied the carving from several sides of the table as she placed the food and motioned for Alberto to be seated. "If Jesu is risen, shouldn't he be smiling?"

Alberto started to scold them and tell them that there is no joy in this world, that only sorrow looks over the shoulder of every poor soul unfortunate enough to live here. Instead he moved one of the candles closer to the figure and studied the face himself. Before he had finished the meal he was plying the fine chisel, scraping and gently scoring the beard, making a smile where before there had been only pain and sorrow. They held the candles while he worked into the evening. Finally he told them he could do no more this day. He thanked the children and sent them on their way with the basket and plates now empty.

After they were gone, he slept well and arose with the morning sun. He made a pot of coffee and began to apply the smoothing stones, sanding and polishing the figure. After the coffee he went to the arroyo where Nolina and Roberto had fallen victim to the flash flood. There he found what he needed, new chunks of sandstone that fit his hand well and had edges that would work for the creases and folds of the robe. He imagined his wife and son struggling to escape the wall of water. He felt the aching of their lungs as the water claimed them. But, somehow, being here helped him to accept their fate, and his loss. He walked back to the house with a commitment to deliver this figure on Easter Sunday.

He worked through the day sanding and smoothing. Often he would pause in his work and wash his hands with the soap Nolina had made last fall so that the figure wouldn't be stained by his sweat. There was still something wrong and by evening, with the setting sun there was still much to do. The folds of the robe still showed the marks of the knife and chisel, the fingers needed to be refined and the feet, the feet. He had completely forgotten the feet.

He answered the knock at the door. This time it was the children of Contessa and Emiglio Alvarez. They owned the farm beyond the canal and raised many cattle. They were, by most standards, the wealthiest people in the community. They were also the most regular in their church attendance. When Father Griego came every other week, he usually stayed with them. The children handed Alberto the sack with several flour tortillas and a half dozen eggs.

"Papa says that we are to bring the sack back to him," the youngest of the children spoke matter of factly. Alberto invited them inside, but they told him they were told not to enter the house because it was probably filthy.

As they turned to leave, the girl handed him a cake of lye. "Mi Madre says that you can use this to clean your clothes before you come to church on Easter Sunday." With this they left.

He closed the door and put the lye on the shelf by the stove. He heated the tortillas and fried two of the eggs. After the meal he put some water on to heat and decided that the white shirt and his patched jeans were the best clothes he had for church. He washed them with the lye and hung them on the line that crossed the room from corner to corner.

After washing the Easter clothes, he sharpened the chisels again and set to work on the feet while the sun cast the long sword-like shadows of evening. He lit the candles the children had brought yesterday and set about carving the feet of Jesu Cristo.

It was then that he noticed that some of the wash water had dripped from his jeans onto the back of the figure. It had turned the wood several shades lighter. At first he was furious with himself for being so careless, then it dawned on him that this was how he could whiten the robe.

Good Friday came and the service was brief but it hit Alberto hard. Christ had suffered for his sins, Christ had to suffer because he, Alberto, and all the other people on earth, had failed. It suddenly, all made sense to him. It also drove him to an understanding of himself, his suffering, his pain and grief.

His life must be devoted to the service of the church, not for his benefit, but to earn salvation for his family; to repay the debt. After the service he returned to his table with renewed energy and determination. The feet were almost finished when the knock at the door distracted him.

This time it was the children of Luis and Marquita Rojas. They entered and set about heating the sliced beef and spring mushrooms on the stove. Melissa poured him a glass of buttermilk and sat the plate of Cross bread before him while Pedrito lit candles made by his mother. Luis was the baker and his sweet breads and Cross cakes were on the table of almost everyone in the village. It was their gift to the church on Easter Sunday as well. They had no money but they shared their bread willingly. These children sat on the bench across from him and chattered as children will do, while they studied his work in the candlelight. Finally they asked if they could touch it. At first he was going to say "NO!" but the look on their faces was so angelic that he consented. Pedrito gently caressed the feet while Melissa stroked the hair.

"I have never seen a santo like this," Pedrito whispered. "Look how fine it is and how the robe is almost white in the candlelight. Could you make his face and hands a little darker, like our skin is?"

"Like this," Melissa said pointing to an old coffee stain on the table.

He dipped a rag in his coffee cup and applied it to a scrap of firewood. It was perfect. The children finally gathered their things and left, thanking him for letting them see, and touch, his santo. He sat and carefully shared his coffee with Jesu Cristo.

Saturday was spent smoothing and polishing, staining and in general making this work as fine and nearly perfect as he could. He labored late into the night, but thoughts of his lost family were never far from his mind. More than once tears fell onto the folds of the robe of Jesu Cristo. Finally exhaustion claimed him and he fell asleep at the table.

The bell was tolling before the sun climbed the mountains to the east. He washed and shaved, dressed in his newly washed clothes and carefully wrapped the broken cross and Jesu

Cristo in the old sheet. After lacing his shoes he gathered his bundle and joined the flow of people as they climbed the hill to the little chapel. Today, every seat was filled.

Alberto handed Father Griego the bundle and entered, claiming a spot on the bench against the back wall.

The statuary was placed before the altar, but left wrapped. The good Father was curious, but hadn't peeked. Nor did any of those gathered have any idea what was concealed in the dusty and tattered sheet. Rumors had made the rounds of the valley, carried by the children for the most part. It was the unveiling that was the incentive for many of the less devout to find their way to the chapel this day.

As the prayers began, the sun streamed through the window and fell on the old sheet. Father Griego was wise enough to keep his comments, both to God and those gathered, brief. Then, with the assistance of two elders the bundle was opened. First the broken cross was struck by the light. Father Griego tried to stand it up straight against the whitewashed altar, but it wouldn't stand. It was fallen and broken. Then they turned their attention to the other figure. As Jesu Cristo was unwrapped, as the sunlight made it glow, the entire congregation gasped in awe.

Never before had they seen a smiling Jesu with his arms reaching up to heaven. What a message of salvation, what a statement of faith. They all turned to thank their santero, but he was not in the chapel. He was almost to the door of his house when someone thought to look outside for him. Father Griego had to change the sermon this Easter Sunday to focus on the joy of the figure before them and the fact that the cross was broken, it had failed to destroy the Son of God.

Then, everyone walked down the hill and stood in the cluttered yard singing hymns to Alberto. An incredible Easter feast was put together in his yard. Everyone complimented Alberto on the quality of his work and the powerful messages that it conveyed. But, he was embarrassed by all the attention. He was unworthy of this praise. Didn't they understand that this was his punishment, the payment for his sins? His only hope was that this had earned him the right to death, an end to the guilt and sorrow that consumed him. The sky was darkening to the west. In the far distance he could see flashes of lightening. He left the gathering and walked down to the arroyo where his family had drowned.

There, in the spot where he thought they must have been when the water came, he knelt and crossed himself. Then he waited. Between intense prayers for deliverance by death and watching the advancing storm, he spent the rest of the afternoon on his knees.

Part three

When the first heavy drops hit his face, he smiled, for the first time in weeks and gave thanks. The lightning was now intense, but the storm was well to the south of the valley. When it passed, there were only the quickly drying spots where an occasional drop had fallen. There was no flash flood, no wall of water that would claim his life and set him free. He cursed God as he stood, and on stiff and aching legs, turned to walk back to the shack he called home.

It was the movement of a blue-tailed lizard that caught his attention, that drew his eyes to the debris trapped from previous angry water. His eyes focused in the roots of the dead juniper, along with the twisted branch leaning against it. It reminded him of a picture in the book of saints in the church. He couldn't remember the saint's name, but he pulled the stump and its roots from the sand and mud. With great difficulty he dragged this dead wood back to his home. Along the way he remembered the name of the saint. It was San Ysidro, the patron saint of the farmers. This santo had been hiding in this stump and he was now calling to Alberto to set him free.

(Author's note: San Ysidro, or Isidro, is the patron saint of agriculture. In Spain he was a field hand, a farm laborer who had been given the difficult task of plowing a stone filled field. When he fell from exhaustion, an angel took up the plow and finished the task.)

It was with an understanding that his penance wasn't yet complete that he set about with the saw to cut the part free that would become San Ysidro, the plowman. The twisted and forked branch that would become the plow was hung above the fireplace. The large piece of stump he carried to the table. But this table was filled with food along with notes of thanks, coins and several tokens of faith. Why didn't they just leave him alone in his guilt and grief, leave him alone to do his penance? But he ate the food, heated a pot of coffee and read each note. The cross carved from a piece of pure white quartz he put around his neck. The miniature painting of the Blessed Virgin he placed on the mantle and the burner with incense he placed on the windowsill.

He tried to sleep. But every time he closed his eyes, he could see the bearded image of San Ysidro trapped in the stump, imploring him to be set free. Finally he rose from the bed and lit the oil lamp, laid out the chisels and set about peeling the bark away and marking the face and arms.

He struggled to remember the story of this saint. As he drew the blade across the wood, the image of the angel plowing the field came to him. He thanked the figure locked within and took the lamp in hand.

In the yard he found what he was looking for. It was in a piece of cedar that he found an angel. He could see it clearly concealed within the robe of bark and silt. He sawed it free and returned to the table. This was going to be a very complex carving. He prayed for the skill to do a santo worthy of both San Ysidro and the church. He fell asleep with chisel in hand.

A routine soon developed. He would rise with the first morning light, put on his coffee or tea, prepare a meager breakfast and set about the work of carving. He would work most of the morning, then walk down to the Sanchez farm and work the fields, pull weeds in the garden or bring water to the animals. Laurisa and Domingo Sanchez never told him what to do, but every Friday afternoon they would give him a few coins, more than they could afford, but they knew that his true labor was for the church. He would immediately spend these coins to buy more oil for the lamp, matches, salt and a bag of candy for the children.

Then he would climb up the hill to his house, build a fire in the stove, heat the coffee and seat himself at the table. The hands were becoming more confident in their efforts. Several times he caught himself humming as he plied the chisels and sanding stones. When he realized this, he would abruptly cease, intensely ashamed of this expression of pleasure and contentment. He was supposed to be suffering as he labored. There wasn't supposed to be any joy involved. Still, he would watch the window. As the sun cast its longest shadows, he would place some of the candy in the chipped and cracked bowl in preparation for what had become another almost daily ritual.

Soon there would be a knock at the door. Two or three of the children from the village would have a sack or basket of food, and always a candle or two. The children would enter and set the table. While Alberto consumed their gift, they would empty the bowl of candy and chatter, as children do so well.

After the meal, they would light the candles and while they illuminated the work, Alberto would ply the tools. They would discuss the role of the saint in their lives, news of the small community and even, on occasion, share a joke or two. These frequent visits from all the children throughout the valley was the high point of the day and Alberto found himself smiling and thanking God for the gift of the children. After the evening's labor, he would take the oil lamp and walk the children back to their home, continuing their conversation until they reached the door. He would then return home and sleep soundly until sunrise.

In the fifty years since this santero began his carving, he had produced an average of one santo, bulto or retablo every month. More than 600 symbols of faith had been produced. Three generations of children carried dinner to his door, and his skill increased with each effort. After fifty years, the children still came. Only, now, with failing eyesight, he could no longer clearly see their smiles.

His work was known far and wide. The faithful from all over the world made the pilgrimage to the Iglesia de Santa Clara de Assisi just to see the incredible assembly of work by a gifted santero. Several of these works had been given to other churches, officials in the church and a few dignitaries. But Alberto never sold a single one. His firm conviction was that there was no way that he should make money from a lifetime of penance.

On numerous occasions he had made special santos for children who had been ill. He created a detailed retablo of the Virgin de Guadalupe for nine year old Maria Cristina Aquinas when she was taken to the hospital in Albuquerque with terminal cancer. Two months later they brought her home and she is still living with her husband and three children in the valley.

Her children knock on the santero's door almost every week. This retablo hangs on the wall of the chapel to this day. The infirm and all of those suffering from pain and sorrow travel hundreds of miles to offer prayers and find comfort in the presence of this work of faith. It is said that there are many miracles that have occurred in this church because of this work alone.

Part four

Alberto is now 87 years old, and almost blind. He would spit and curse that he must now see with his hands. But those hands are still strong and possess the skill learned in over half a century of labor. Father Griego's hearing is poor and he walks with a cane, but he still visits this church faithfully, two days every month.

It was after worship on Sunday, November 1, All Saints Day, when the children asked if they could do a special Christmas program for the church and entire community. They wanted to do a Posada and create a nativity in the church yard. They asked him if he could carve the figures for this life size Navidad.

In fifty years as a santero this was the first time anyone had asked him to do a specific subject. This was also one of the biggest projects he had ever contemplated.

He slowly walked down the hill to the shack that had been his home and studio all these years. He sat at the table, eyes closed and hands folded, and prayed. He prayed for guidance. He was a frail old man and this was a monumental task. Next, he prayed for insight, then for strength. Finally, he prayed to God and all the saints for help. The afternoon light came through the window in golden shafts as the sun fell closer to the mountains in the west. The Lady of the Light came to mind, his very first effort, his first santo. He smiled at his lack of understanding then. His mind roamed through the hundreds of pieces of wood that he had worked, the multitude of santos and bultos he had liberated from the scraps and the firewood, fallen trees and dead branches.

"How strange it is that you have used this useless scrap of humanity to turn scraps of wood into symbols of faith and reverence," he whispered to God. His conversation was interrupted by a knock at the door.

"Senor Alberto," almost twenty children spoke at once as he opened the door, "We want to help you make the Navidad. Will you let us? Will you teach us how to carve the wood?"

He smiled and looked toward the heavens, "I guess you have answered me. This must be el destino." Then he invited all of the children inside. While he passed out the candy, they began to plan the Navidad for the Iglesia de Santa Clara de Assisi.

By the first Sunday in November they had gathered most of the wood they needed. Alberto, with the aid of a cane roamed the hillsides, always with three or four of the children. They found fallen pinon and juniper that could be used for the animals and the creche. They spent a great deal of time peeling the bark, trimming and placing these so that this Navidad would be visible from every home in the valley below. But there were no logs large enough for the wise men, the shepherds or the holy family itself.

On that Sunday Father Griego arrived in a truck loaded with small logs. Many of the men and women of the valley gathered at the church to help unload them. The afternoon was spent trimming and standing each of these logs where that figure was to be standing, or kneeling. In all there were ten figures, The Virgin Mary, Joseph, three Kings, three shepherds and two angels.

It was Alberto's primary goal this afternoon to read each of these pieces of wood with his hands, and decide who was inside each log waiting for the liberating chisel and knife. He slowly moved down the line of logs, caressing each with his hands and studying with clouded eyes that refused to focus. Still he was able to mark rough pencil lines on each as the figure revealed itself to him.

The children had the bark trimmed away and had started the rough shaping by the time the setting sun called an end to their labors. But no one wanted to leave. Parents brought food, and neighbors lit fires for light and warmth. The choir began to sing the hymns of the approaching season after the meal and the entire community joined in the building of the creche. Father Griego napped in the church. Then he led prayers through the evening as each of the logs was worked by two or three of the children. Alberto slowly moved from figure to figure pointing out with his pencil or finger where a fold of a robe needed to be, or where the feet would be freed from the wood.

It was after ten before the children tired. Parents led them home to bed, but Alberto stayed in the dwindling light of the fires, struggling to turn figures, marking details to be worked the next afternoon after school, and marking where each of the animals would be placed when the time came. Then he gathered the tools and slowly walked down the hill to his shack, lit the oil lamp and sharpened the tools until he fell asleep at the grinding wheel.

In the first rays of dawn he was back on the hill studying the light and shadows, with his aged and cloudy eyes, moving the figures ever so slightly to catch the greatest illumination. In his mind he could see every subtle nuance of light on the people within these logs, even though not a single face was even marked out yet. His cataracts grew worse by the day and he sometimes stumbled, but he had a vision of what this was to be and he would not be deterred.

By the time the children returned, he had each figure marked with what was to be accomplished that day. Parents brought supper to their children and their santero. Fires were lit again and everyone wandered among the figures studying the progress and admiring the artistry.

The Atrisco children, Angelina and Bartolo, early showed the most skill and dedication. Bartolo had a true reverence for the wood and the work. He was even confident enough that he would question Alberto's marks and lines on occasion. Alberto had on several occasions made errors just to see if Bartolo would notice, and he always did. Sometimes Bartolo would ignore Alberto's lines and follow his own inspiration. Angelina was skillful with the chisel and sanding stone, never working too fast, never showing the least impatience with herself or the task. Of all the children that had become a part of this project, these two, Alberto knew in his heart, would become the next generation of santeros.

It was on November 13th when the accident happened. No one saw him fall. In the noise and confusion of the children and the faithful wielding chisels and mallets, singing and eating, no one heard him call for help. Alberto had gone down the hill to the pile of wood, stumps, branches and roots stacked against the side of his house. In pulling a piece of root free from the rest he fell, breaking his right leg and shattering the ankle. Soon the children missed him and lit torches to find him. When he was found, they carried him to the church and placed him under the retablo of the Virgin de Guadeloupe.

There Frieda, the village curandera, set the bones and gave him a tea that eased the pain and made him sleep. Several women of the community stayed with him that night in the church, and in the morning he was carried to a truck and driven down the hill to the Alvarez house. There he was well cared for and while the healing was slow, his bones did knit. The curandera used her herbs, healing mud packs and incense to keep him calm and encourage the mending.

It was the next day, in the bar that his old friends from his wild days were talking, that an idea was born. It was agreed that they would get all the men of the valley together and repair his shack of a house, put new siding on it, fix the roof, paint the walls and get him new furniture. The women cleaned, scrubbed the wooden floors and painted the pantry, which was then stocked with an abundance of food. Bartolo and Angelina carved a pair of crutches for him. The children took turns visiting him and bringing progress reports about the Navidad, but not a word was mentioned about what was being done to his home.

He was worried about the project, and was desperate to have it completed by Christmas Eve, but it bothered him most that he had let the children down. Ten days later he was driven to the church where he struggled with the crutches but managed to examine each of the figures.

The children, Angelina and Bartolo in particular, had every day walked from the school to the church on the hill to carve and saw and chisel. They shared his vision and wanted to make him proud of them. They had followed the lines he had drawn to make the robes and even the sandals on the feet. Angelina had begun sanding and smoothing the sleeves, even though the hands were still blocks of wood, unmarked. Mary and Joseph were kneeling and the manger was already filled with straw. The shepherds were standing and the wise men were at the side looking on, waiting impatiently to be set free of the wood that bound them. The angels were one on each side, waiting for their wings. All were waiting for Alberto to give them eyes to see and a mouth to proclaim the event.

He began with the shepherds, carefully marking where the chisel was to be applied. Then, while Angelina and Bartolo held his crutches, he used the light mallet and the finest chisel to show them how to use these guide lines to set each one completely free.

In the fifty years as a santero he had never worked with anything this large. Yet he dare not show any lack of confidence. The pain in his leg and foot were eased when he was brought a cup of hot tea. The children took turns holding him up as he went from figure to figure. He studied carefully the work they had done and was pleased.

Finally, he sat on the chair one of them had brought for him. With bowed head he thanked God for guiding the hands of these children as his own had been guided. It was the time of the day when shadows play tricks on the vision, especially the vison of an old man. He asked one of the children to bring a candle so that he could see better the details that all agreed only he could create.

First one, then another, and another returned from the chapel with a candle. As the darkness fell, two children helped him to stand while he was surrounded by all the others. Each was holding a candle, illuminating the artistry, every line, every stroke of his hands. Because his sight was failing, these candles were the only way he could hope to complete this, his ultimate work as a santero. The first night he completed the face of the first of the shepherds before becoming so weak he could no longer hold the chisel or the sanding stone.

The children almost carried him down the hill to his house. This was the first he had seen what the community had done for him. The new siding and paint glowed in the candlelight. When the door was opened, he was overwhelmed. On the table was a fine meal. A welcoming fire burned in the fireplace and the oil lamp was burning brightly. It was almost beyond his understanding. "Who has done all this?" he asked. "And why?"

The curtain that hung over the doorway into the other room was parted and Father Griego led a group of friends into the light. They seated him at the table that had been scarred with a multitude of chisel and knife marks, and served him a feast. Then they brought out packages of new clothes, brand new boots and a retablo created by Angelina and Bartolo that showed the church and the figures of the Navidad. The work was ill proportioned and obviously not professional, but there was a warmth and devotion to it that brought tears to Alberto's eyes. It was Father Griego who, leaning on his cane, pointed to the figure of a santero working on one of the wise men. It was several moments before Alberto realized that he was looking at himself at work. There was much applause and laughter from everyone present, except Alberto.

There were tears in his eyes, tears that escaped and trailed down his cheek, through his moustache and onto his chin. He tried to stand, but could not. Finally he shouted with as much strength as he could muster, "Silencio! Silencio!"

As the room fell silent, he cleared his throat and spoke very softly. "I do not deserve all this. I am only the town drunk who killed his family with neglect. All these carvings that I have done were penance. I have spent a lifetime in paying for my sins. This is not the kind of labor deserving of praise, or gifts."

He was going to continue but the aged priest interrupted. "Alberto, what you view as punishment, we all see as a gift. The santos you created are used every week to teach these children the very foundations of their faith, and by those adults here and in the rest of this valley as reminders of what is good, and what being a devout Christian is about."

He stepped forward, opened a scroll and read from it.

"In honor of the lifetime devotion to the Iglesia de Clara de Assisi and the artistry you have shown in honoring God, Jesu Cristo and the Holy Virgin, and all the saints by producing more than six hundred bultos, santos and retables, we the parishioners of said church do hereby bestow the title of DON upon you.

You are henceforth to be known as Don Alberto and shall be treated with the appreciation and respect that rightfully accompanies this title. We furthermore proclaim that as long as you shall live you shall never want for food, warmth, shelter or the support of true friends."

A title of Don is a symbol of respect and is given usually to the most successful members of the community, not the poorest. Don Alberto was speechless. After the children and the visitors departed for the night, he discovered his new bed with a real mattress and brand new, hand sewn quilts to keep him warm. He thanked God again for the gifts and added, "It is good to know that one has friends."

The morning sun came through the window, as it always had. And there sitting at the table was Bartolo. He helped the old man from his bed and prepared a good breakfast, complete with fresh coffee. While they were slowly making the climb up the hill, several of the other children joined them. Work was slow that day. Alberto had to stop frequently and warm his hands by the fire and rest his broken leg.

By evening most of the children were there with their candles, and while Alberto and Bartolo and Angelina did the detail work, the rest of the children held their candles close and sang songs of the season.

This became the cycle of days for that last week. Often Alberto would have to stop and rest, but the shepherds, the wise men and Mary and Joseph were all completed. The angels and the Infanto were all that was left.

Three days to Christmas Eve Angelina worked the wings from pieces of cottonwood found in the carpenter's shed. They had been warped by nature and time to give the image of life and motion. After she had carved them to shape and incised the feathers, they looked as though they could take flight. Exhausted, they gathered, wrapping the Infanto and all those in the Navidad in an embrace of pure love and peace.

Bartolo worked the hair and hands of the angels while Alberto, now always with the light from dozens of candles smoothed the angelic cheeks, gave life to the eyes and curved the lips into joyous smiles.

It was the evening of December 23 and all that was left was the Infanto to be placed in the manger. Alberto had selected the perfect piece of cedar, a tree sacred to the local Indians. Bartolo brought it into the house so that he could work on it at the table.

It was slightly curved as a baby sleeping would be. He began with the chisel and mallet but his arms were no longer strong enough to swing this tool. He would hold the chisel in place as Angelina and Bartolo took turns with the heavy wooden hammer.

By early evening the rough form was taking shape. Twice Alberto had fallen asleep with tools in his hands. He was exhausted and his leg was causing him a great deal of pain.

Angelina and Bartolo let him sleep. Together they did the shaping and smoothed the folds in the blanket of the carving. Alberto awoke, little refreshed, but he returned to the labors. The face with its most delicate smile and the eyes that were closed in peaceful slumber were finished at about the same time the sun fell behind the western hills.

61

Then Angelina and Bartolo carried it up the hill to the waiting children. Their candles lit the way to the manger and Alberto followed with assistance from several of the others. They worked late into the night making certain that every detail was as close to perfect as could be.

Finally, one by one the children departed. It was obvious that Alberto was exhausted and needed rest. They led the way to his house with their candles and helped him to his bed.

There in the darkness and silence of the night before Christmas Eve, Alberto slept more soundly than he had in fifty years. The morning sun streamed through the window, yet he did not stir. Angelina entered and began preparing breakfast for him, but even the sounds of cooking did not awaken him.

Finally she went to his bed and called to him.

He opened his eyes, blinked and shouted, "I can see!" He began to pull himself to a sitting position while Angelina reached for his crutches, but he was on his feet before she could return.

She ran from his house shouting "It's a miracle! We have seen a Miracle! Viemos el milagro!"

Soon others from the community arrived to see Alberto standing at the doorway. His smile was broader than anyone could remember.
"I have been forgiven my sins. I can see, I can walk, I can laugh!" he kept saying over and over again. "Praise God. I have been forgiven."

That night he led the way for the entire community from the valley to the church, the way being lit by all the children holding their candles.

Most would expect that the story ends with Don Alberto passing away on Christmas Day, but the facts are a little different.

He lived to be almost a hundred and apprenticed both Bartolo and Angelina. They have continued his tradition of making the most detailed and carefully crafted santos. And every Christmas the Navidad that the children of the community created so many years ago now, is placed at the entrance to the old church.

There has only been one change in all those years. The two apprentices carved another shepherd, who looks a lot like Don Alberto, the Santero of their valley.

The Little People in the Attic

a Christmas story from Roswell, NM

Roswell, the county seat of Chavez County, NM, is a modest town built by hard working people who came west to seek a new life, others who stumbled upon a new continent and were enchanted by the land here, and some folks who had ancestors familiar with this land before we began counting time. Farming, ranching, and the fine art of living are the traditions and the legacy of this place. But history often denies us what is a supposed destiny. Dr. Goddard began this journey toward a different kind of destiny for the people of Roswell in the 1930's when he started launching rockets in the nearby desert.

In 1941 Walker Air Force Base was commissioned and a test pilot and instructor, Henry John Deutschendorf Sr. was an officer there. On December 31, 1943, Henry and Erma Deutschendorf had a son they named Henry John Deutschendorf, Jr., but we know him as the folk singer, humanitarian and environmentalist, John Denver. During WWII this area was the site of a Prisoner of War camp where German inmates constructed much of the infrastructure of Roswell. Much of their legacy remains today.

After the war things were quiet in Roswell,that is until July 2, 1947 when something occurred during a thunderstorm. A crash of some sort over seventy miles from Roswell gave the media something to talk about, speculate upon and develop some very creative stories about. Some said it was the crash of a flying saucer and insisted that several bodies of little green men had been recovered. Others said that it was a weather balloon. The truth is often not as exciting as fiction, but after all these years, as is the case with much of the history of this planet we call home, the truth has been revealed.

I feel a twinge of guilt sharing this with you, but as a writer I am driven to "spill the beans." This is the way the story was told to me, and all I can do is ask you to swear yourself to secrecy. Please do not tell another living soul what I am about to share. The joy and happiness of the children of the world is now in your hands. Please, keep this just between the two of us.

Part one

This was one of those bleak Christmases for Christina and Chad, and their four year old daughter, Erika, whose nickname was Elf. We have all known such a season, filled with sadness and gloom. Often that Christmas becomes the most fondly remembered, perhaps because in the hard times the truth of the season shines the brightest. So often we fear tomorrow. We carry the burden of guilt, convinced that we have failed those we love the most. This may not be our fault, but we are the ones who feel the pain.

Still, events carry us forward. Some doors are slammed shut, but usually other doors open, or at least they're unlocked. Events beyond our control provide challenges and opportunities, cause tears and smiles. Sometimes we just have to hold on tightly, and sometimes we have to let go lightly. The glitz and glamour of the marketplace always leave us either unsatisfied, or dissatisfied. But sometimes the best gift is a good question, even when that answer must remain a secret. This story is based on such a question. We ask you to keep the answer a secret.

It all started that bleak, cold, cloudy day they moved into the old abandoned farmhouse. It was the first day of December 2008. Christina tried so hard to be a good sport about this move from Albuquerque to Roswell, but it wasn't her choice.

Nor was this what Chad would have chosen, but these were difficult times for everyone. Chad had been on the assembly line at Eclipse Aviation. This was the company that was going to revolutionize air travel. That was until they went belly up when the economy tanked. Her job evaporated a month later when the Linens & Things store decided to go out of business. Part time jobs failed to pay the bills or nourish the spirit. These odd jobs were short lived and the paychecks didn't come in an envelope labeled "HOPE."

Still Elf, at the age of four, thought this was a grand adventure. She sat in her car seat and watched the scenery rush by as they approached their new home.

Perhaps I should explain. It was a week before Thanksgiving that Christina received the registered letter from the attorney. It came two traumatic, tear-filled days after the foreclosure notice. Just as they were about to lose their Albuquerque dream home, there was this ray of hope. It seemed that Christina was the last surviving heir of a distant uncle she could barely remember. Tio Marti had an old farm just east of Roswell. Decades ago he leased the land to a rancher nearby and lived basically on the whiskey and beans the rent money provided. She had been notified when he had passed away a couple years ago, but couldn't recall what he looked like.

Actually he died in the bed of his ancient pickup parked in front of the convenience store after consuming his liquid purchase from the night before.

He had been to the Roswell Police Department filing a complaint about his house being haunted. Now it should be noted that he didn't live in the old farmhouse anymore. It was too far from the source of his liquid nourishment. He would visit the old farm occasionally to look for something else to pawn, but he was afraid to live there. This was Roswell after all, and he was certain that the aliens from the flying saucer crash in 1947 were still there. He told everyone they were still looking for unsuspecting victims they could stun with their lasers and take back to where ever it was they came from for study. Or perhaps they were just ghosts. As much as he drank, he saw lots of ghosts. Residents of Roswell joked that these ghosts escaped from the bottled spirits he emptied with such regularity.

Officer Rodriguez dutifully recorded his complaint on the proper forms and filed this paperwork in the proper pile on the cluttered desk. "We'll get someone out there as soon as we can," he said, dismissing the old man with something between a smile and a smirk.

After the low end funeral, the people of Roswell pretty much forgot all about Marti. The cattle were the only visitors to the old farm house. When no one paid the electric bill, the power company shut off the electricity. It was just another abandoned house on a farm so dry even the tumbleweed struggled to escape. Now, this letter told her that whatever was left of it was theirs.

After the final meeting with the lawyer, they drove the 200 miles to the abandoned farmhouse just outside the world famous city of Roswell. The 100 miles down I-285 were filled with active, though not always positive conversation, and a good deal of apprehension. Chad attempted to lighten the gloom by joking about the old farmhouse being the headquarters for Roswell's extraterrestrials. But his wife didn't see the humor as tears ran down her cheeks.

Elf viewed this with childish enthusiasm. Christina didn't agree. "I'm a city girl," she moaned, "What am I gonna do out here without a friend in cell phone range and not a neighbor in sight?"

Chad was most worried about making a living, but was thankful that at least they would have a roof over their heads and a place to call home, at least until the economy turned around. However, when they finally arrived, even this was doubtful. The old house looked so forlorn. The dismal, dark clouds made the building look a little less than livable.

The fact that there was neither electricity nor DSL didn't help Christina's mood. She sat in the aging Subaru clutching her laptop, her connection to the rest of the world, which now seemed so remote they might as well be on Mars. The tears continued to flow, even though she clenched her teeth and tried to be brave.

Elf, on the other hand, was awestruck. "Wow!" she said as she climbed out of her car seat. "Wow, just like one of my storybooks. Is this a haunted house?"

Part two

They unloaded the boxes and garbage bags containing their meager possessions and piled them inside the door. Then they returned to Roswell to get the power turned on. It was late afternoon when they returned. They set to work turning the empty house into a home as best they could. Some of the windows were broken and the desert winds had carried so much sand into this old house they could have played a good game of beach volleyball in the living room.

Making this place livable would take days, weeks perhaps, maybe even months, if ever again it could be called a home. This afternoon it meant hours of sweeping and shoveling the sand out the back door. This was an emergency cleanup, serious cleaning would have to wait.

Chad noticed in the fading light of a tired sun retreating below the distant hills, what appeared to be tiny footprints in the sand near the back door. He followed them across the living room and to the steps leading up to the attic.

"Don't. Please don't." Christina pleaded as Chad, armed with the shovel he found outside the kitchen door, started up the creaking steps. "It's too dark." Her voice trembled with fear. He decided she was right and returned to the living room.

"Please don't hurt them." Elf said tugging on Daddy's shirt sleeve.

He agreed with only a moment's hesitation, and put the shovel back by the kitchen door. Still, he frequently glanced toward the stairs, and the tracks in the sand and dust. Fear is even worse when you can't admit it, when you have to appear strong and brave.

Wearing dust masks they had thought to buy in Roswell, they finished sweeping the mouse nests out of what was once the kitchen, and set up the card table and folding chairs they had brought with them. It was long after dark, but, with the light from the oil lamp they found on the fireplace mantle, they continued cleaning until they were all too exhausted to do any more. Finally, they crawled into their sleeping bags. Elf was giggling. For her this was an adventure, like their camping trips to remote places in the mountains and the desert. It was cold without the furnace, but the sleeping bags were warm. Finally sleep came for all of them.

Elf heard it first. A soft tap-tap-tap, so faint she wasn't certain at first that she had heard anything at all. It seemed to be coming from the attic. Then Christina heard something, a noise like something being pulled across the floor. More taps and strange mechanical sounds awoke Chad. Memories of the stories Tio Marti had told amplified these sounds and provided mental images that neither wanted to see. Silently, almost afraid to breathe, they waited for what seemed like hours.

There were other sounds from outside. They seemed to match those coming from the attic. Then there were the sounds old wooden stairs make, the squeaks and groans, when feet are going up and down them. Chad sat up and searched for the flashlight. Christina whispered that now she could hear voices. They all held their breath and listened as hard as they could. Yes, it did sound like almost human voices, but high pitched, and there seemed to be laughter as well. Christina found her clothes while Chad fumbled in the dark continuing his quest for one of the flashlights, but it was not where he had left it. Elf sat on the middle of her sleeping bag, eyes shut tightly so she could hear better. She was smiling and humming along to some imaginary tune.

They all dressed as quickly and quietly as they could in the dark and raced to the safety of the car. Once inside they locked the doors and sat watching the house. They dozed fitfully until there was the hint of morning in the predawn sky. In this dim light they cautiously walked back to the old outhouse. Chad clutched the flashlight from the car's glove compartment like a weapon. He was prepared to defend his family against whatever it was in there.

On the way Christina pointed to what appeared to be skid marks in the dirt outside the back door. There were also tracks of some hoofed animal. "Might be pronghorns," Chad whispered, "too small for cattle." He was afraid to mention that these skid marks could be the landing pads of a flying saucer. All his jokes about Roswell didn't seem as funny now.

Elf just smiled at her parents, but didn't say a word. They just wouldn't understand. After all, they were grownups. There are some things only a child knows.

They followed these tracks until they simply disappeared, both the skid marks and the hoof prints. "This never-ending wind might have erased them." Chad explained as he knelt to study them in the faint light of a new day.

Christina stepped back and tried to smooth Elf's windblown hair with her fingers. Then she spoke, half joking, half in earnest. "What if it's a flying saucer? What if Tio Marti was right?" They retreated to the car to wait for the morning sun to bring them courage.

Daylight came as they shared a breakfast of peanut butter and jelly sandwiches in the car. Now, with the courage the sun brings, they reentered the house. Piled in the middle of the floor were all three of their sleeping bags. Each neatly folded. There was a fire in the wood stove and a blue spatter ware pot sat on top, filled with steaming hot coffee. On the card table were two coffee mugs, a glass of orange juice and a plate of Christmas cookies.

Chad cautiously searched every room but found no clues as to who might have built the fire or made the coffee. Finally convinced that there was no one there, Christina poured the coffee while Elf sampled one of the cookies. Both were delicious.

It was almost noon before they found the courage to venture up the stairs. Chad led the way, clutching the shovel. Christina followed closely behind, muttering prayers almost forgotten, from childhood, from the dim memories of Sunday mornings when Abuelita Elaina would take her to early mass. As they neared the top of the stairs, Elf raced past them.

"Cool!" she shouted as she disappeared through the doorway.

There were three rooms in this upstairs. In each were rows of tables barely two feet off the floor, each surrounded by child size chairs. Craft tools, scissors and such, filled racks on the walls of the first room, along with boxes overflowing with all sorts of wiggle eyes. In the corner was a mountain of stuffing, bags of teddy bear ears and rolls of faux fur in every color of the rainbow. The scent of clean clothes, line dried in the sunshine, and the hint of perfumes from decades past made Christina smile as images of Abuletia Elaina's famous quilting bees flashed through her mind.   Elf picked out a teddy bear from the pile and hugged it tightly. "See. I told you not to hurt them. This is where they make all the teddy bears." It all seemed so perfectly logical to this little girl.

The second room was filled with stacks of wood, cans of paint, pots of glue, wood & plastic wheels, train cars and airplane wings. Hammers, saws, pliers and paint brushes were neatly hung on the pegboard along the back wall. The delightful fragrance of sawdust and fresh paint hung in the air. These triggered memories in Chad's mental attic, memories of his grandfather's basement shop. There was comfort, even a little reassurance, in these scents. But the big questions still remained. Who was doing all this? What was going on here?

Christina led the way to the third room, her fear now completely replaced by curiosity. The most alluring aromas hit them as they neared the doorway. White dust covered the tables and the floor. Miniature ovens, looking for all the world like something from a child's toy kitchen, lined the back wall. Stacks of boxes in bright colors lined another wall, while sacks of flour, sugar, spices and so much more were piled in the middle of the floor. On a large table along the far wall were stacks of mixing bowls, cookie sheets, wooden spoons and cookie cutters in every imaginable shape. Tiny chefs' hats and aprons were hung on pegs just inside the door.

Elf sampled one of the star shaped cookies that seemed to be waiting on the table just for her. "Delicious!" she said licking her lips.

She held the plate out to Mommy and Daddy, "Try one." Of course they did, and soon the plate was empty, except for a few crumbs.

Chad pointed to the boxes filled with cookies sitting on the nearest table. They were just like the ones they had found downstairs. "What's going on here?"

"Well, I don't think it's a bunch of Martians making teddy bears and baking Christmas cookies." Christina said as she began straightening and stacking the boxes of cookies on the table. Then she stepped back. With fear in her voice she whispered, "What if they are a part of some drug cartel and this is the way they're smuggling something into the country?"

"I don't think drug dealers or illegal aliens would make coffee and leave a plate of cookies for us." Chad responded, but he too backed away from the table and took Elf by the hand as they made their way back to the stairs.

Soon they were sitting at the card table again, trying to understand all this. "The skid marks might have been from a flying saucer." Chad speculated, looking for some other, perhaps safer, option than drug dealers.

"I think that's carrying our fear of illegal aliens a bit too far." Christina said as she examined the cookie clutched in her hand. "Even if the flavor of these is out of this world, I doubt they were baked by a Martian Rachel Ray."

"But what about all the little tables and stools, and those miniature aprons? And why did they fold up our sleeping bags for us? Why would they, whoever they are, build a fire in that old stove and make us a pot of delicious coffee?" Chad wondered out loud.

Elf walked over to her box of books and sat down to read Teddy a story. Several times she glanced at her parents, but all she could do was shake her head. They were too grown up to understand.

Christina looked into Chad's eyes, "I'm not sure I want to stay here anymore, but I don't think whoever, or whatever, they are, I don't think they mean us any harm. Do they?"

After finishing the coffee and most of the cookies on the plate, they walked out the back door. Chad wanted to walk around the house again. A new multitude of tiny footprints covered the bare earth outside the back door, and new hoof prints seemed to be going in all directions, along with a new series of skid marks.

They continued their walk around this old building, past the tracks, then over to the barn, with its swayback roof collapsing under the weight of neglect. There standing guard in front of the barn door was what looked just like a garden Gnome. Christina gasped and clutched Elf's hand tightly. Then they both laughed as they realized that it was nothing more than a chipped and faded old lawn ornament. But the real surprise was inside the barn. There were hundreds more of these gnomes, in all sizes and shapes. Most were reclining in the straw, but a few were standing or leaning against bales of hay. There were pots of patching plaster, cans of paint, brushes and sculpting tools neatly lined up on several worn and scarred tables. Several of the Gnomes were lying on what reminded Chad of operating tables with obvious plaster patches drying in the arid atmosphere. Each one had taped to its hand a card with something written on it in a script they couldn't decipher.

"Someone has set up a Gnome hospital," Elf quipped as she examined these 'patients' more closely.

"This is the weirdest thing I have ever seen." Chad commented as he carefully touched one of the newly painted Gnomes. "Was this your uncle's hobby?"

Christina laughed out loud. "Maybe he's the one to blame when your garden gnomes disappear."

They returned to the house and continued the cleanup until they had swept out the last of the kangaroo rat and deer mouse nests, and even stacked more firewood by the wood stove in the kitchen. Then without a word Elf went out to the wood pile and gathered an armload of small sticks and pieces of wood. This she carried up the stairs and neatly piled by the mini ovens in the baking room.

They returned to Roswell to get some groceries and, as they were checking out, they entered into a conversation with the cashier. Chad mentioned that they were moving into the old Marti Lopez farm house and that he was available for odd jobs in town.

She backed away and whistled, "You know that place is haunted don't you?" She finished bagging their purchase in silence. Then, as they were folding up the receipt she added, "Folks around here are afraid to go near that place. Rumor has it your uncle was killed by whatever it is that's lurkin' out there."

Chad started to reply, "Tio Marti was killed by spirits all right, but it was the kind hiding in a bottle. I don't think those . . ."

Christina grabbed him by the arm and completed his sentence. "What he means is that since we don't drink we aren't afraid of demon rum, or whiskey for that matter. Thank you for the warning though."

That night they were still without electricity, but the old house was at least clean. They dined on canned tamales and refritos heated on the wood stove. It was decided that they would take turns staying awake to see who their visitors were. But Elf was asleep the minute she climbed into her sleeping bag.

Christina drew the first watch and lay in her sleeping bag absolutely still. Then she heard the sounds outside the window. It was as if a herd of cattle was rushing past. Then there was a sliding sound, followed by silence, except for what might have been whispers and giggles. Someone, or something was obviously outside the back door, and they were having a good time. Christina climbed out of the sleeping bag and picked up the flashlight. Her plan was to go to the window, then turn the flashlight on and solve this little mystery once and for all.

Before she got to the window though, she heard a sound in the kitchen. Now she was frightened again and returned to the sleeping bags to wake Chad. By the time he opened his eyes, the scurrying up and down the stairs had stopped and there was another rush of hooves in the dry earth outside. Chad gathered Elf in his arms, sleeping bag and all.

Together they walked into the kitchen. In the moonlight they could see something large sitting on the card table. It also appeared that someone was sitting on the chairs. Chad grabbed the shovel in his right hand and clutched the flashlight in the left. Christina held the flashlight and Elf's hand, both as securely as she could. They advanced through the doorway, aimed their flashlights at the mystery on the table, then together they turned them on.

Part three

There on the table was a huge tumbleweed, painted green and white with assorted Christmas cookies hanging all over it. Seated on the folding chairs were three of the garden Gnomes from the barn. Each still had the tag taped to its hand.

They could do nothing else but burst into uncontrollable laughter. Finally, Chad regained control of himself and gave Christina and Elf a hug. "Gotta admit, those Martians sure do have a sense of humor that's out of this world."

"They aren't Martians," Elf said quietly. She would have told them more, but they were too old to understand.

Christina led the way out the back door. There were new skid marks and another cluster of hoof tracks that just seemed to end about thirty feet from where it appeared something had landed.

It was agreed that the next night they would stay in the car and watch for whatever it was that seemed to make a nightly visit. After another busy day of fixing and patching, sanding and preparing to paint, they were exhausted. Dinner was a package of Ramen noodles and a salad, which was devoured with the enthusiasm of a gourmet meal. Darkness arrived early with a brief shower and a cold wind. They retreated to the car and wrapped themselves in blankets to wait.

Unfortunately they all quickly fell asleep, and slept soundly the whole night through. When they awoke at dawn they quickly returned to the house and, sure enough, there on the wood stove was a fresh pot of coffee. A platter of fresh baked biscochitos sat on the table beside the tumbleweed Christmas tree. There were also several gourds hanging on the tumbleweed tree in front of the smiling Gnomes. Each was hand painted in a variety of southwest symbols, scenes and themes.

They shared the coffee and the cookies. Then they climbed the stairs to the workshop. This time Elf led the way. Now there were stacks of teddy bears, all different colors and sizes along the walls of the first room. Piles of cloth, cut into various sizes and styles of doll clothes filled the tables to almost overflowing.

The second room was covered, both floor and tables, with wooden cars, trucks and trains all recently painted and still drying. Stacks of wooden blocks sat near box after box of brightly colored model airplanes.

A most delightful aroma emanated from the third room, the bakery. Stacks of cinnamon and anise scented biscochitos covered the tables.

"Whoever is doing this is doing it for a reason." Chad was sounding skeptical. Elf was sitting at one of the knee high tables completing a jigsaw puzzle that had been left about half done. It was covered with images of brightly colored fairies and hummingbirds. Christina was also trying to piece all this together in her mind, but too many pieces of her puzzle were missing.

"Chad," she said as they carefully made their way back to the stairs amidst the piles of toys and foods. "Chad, didn't we see an old elevator sitting behind the barn?"

Chad confirmed this with a confused look on his face. Elf was reluctant to leave before she had completed her puzzle, but Chad insisted. They made their way down the stairs and out to the barn. This time a huge Gnome pushing a wheelbarrow greeted them by the barn door. The wheelbarrow was filled with small round and pear shaped gourds. There was a piece of paper taped to the handle of the wheelbarrow. In a most curious script it read "Start with these. More will follow. Then in spring you can grow your own."

"Mommy, Daddy, we can make Christmas tree ornaments, just like the ones on the table," Elf shouted as she began sorting through them.

"That does sound like fun," Chad laughed, then picked up one of the more unusual shaped ones and began envisioning what images it called for.

They walked to the back of the barn and examined the ancient elevator, designed to lift bales of hay to the loft. Chad tinkered with it for a few minutes before he turned to Christina with a smile on his face. "It's old, but with a little oil it will probably work. Think we can sell it?"

She put her hand on his shoulder. When he turned around, she hugged him and gave him a big kiss. "No, you dummy. Can we pull it over to the attic window?"

"Sure, but . . . But, what are you thinking?"

"Cool," Elf squealed as she jumped up on the machine, "Can I ride it?"

Chad laughed and picked her up. After a hug he sat her on the ground, "No, but you can help push this over to the house."

They all struggled to push, pull and drag the machine across the barnyard, but it barely budged. Finally, Christina sat on the ground and leaned against the stubborn machine. "Whoever they are, whatever they are, they have been nice to us. If we can help them get their stuff up and down from that attic workshop it could be a way to say thanks."

"Can we pull it with the car?" Elf asked as she climbed back onto the elevator.

In a matter of minutes it was parked by the back of the house. Before an hour passed they had the rusted old piece of machinery oiled and ready to move whatever it was that whoever it was had been carrying up and down the stairs.

"How do you power it?" Christina asked as she wiped the oil from her hands.

"It's easy. All we need is a tractor."

"But, we don't have one." Elf said, trying to figure out what they were up to now.

As Christina sat down in the dust amidst the hoof tracks, she spotted a burro walking out from behind the barn. "How about him?"

In a matter of minutes they had a rope around the poor little beast's neck and were leading it to the well for a drink of water. Christina disappeared, but soon returned with several carrots and half a head of cabbage. Instantly, she made a friend for life. Chad spent the rest of the afternoon devising a harness and a series of gears that would turn the elevator belt when the burro walked in a circle. Chad had been an engineering student at UNM, and while not at the head of his class, he easily mastered this problem.

Christina had grown up on a farm and her father had an ancient and cantankerous Oliver tractor. She suggested that this might be the perfect name for their new-found friend. They fastened the rope harness to Oliver. Then, with carrot in hand Elf led Oliver around the newly formed track. With a bit more tinkering the old elevator worked well, even though it did squeak and groan as the gears turned.

Satisfied with their afternoon's labor, they returned to the house and snacked on the cookies. It was decided that they would return to Roswell for a few more groceries before dark. They started out the door, but Christina paused and turned back to the kitchen.

"Forget something?" Chad called to her while he and Elf continued to the car.

She held up several of the painted gourd ornaments in her hands as she reappeared in the doorway. "I want to see if there is a market for these."

72

Part four

The drive back to Roswell was spent trying to decide what they should say about the Gnomes in the barn and what was going on in their attic.

Elf sat in her car seat with a perplexed look on her face. Finally she spoke. "They won't understand either," then she smiled and added, "Just like you. They are all too grownup to believe."

Finally, they agreed that it would be best if they simply kept silent about all that was happening, at least until they could figure out just what it was that was happening.

They parked at the Smiths Supermarket. While Chad and Elf started threading the shopping cart through the grocery store, Christina took the gourd ornaments to the Alien Landing Pad Gift Shop next door to the grocery. In a matter of minutes she had traded the six painted gourd ornaments for thirty dollars and promised to deliver a couple dozen more within a week.

Chad laughed out loud when she caught up with them in the produce aisle and showed him her "gourd money."

It was after they put the groceries in the car and started down the street that Christina spied the As Good as New Second Hand Store. Inside they found a real bed for ten dollars and a dresser that almost matched for another ten dollars. The real wood kitchen table was marked $9.00 and the elderly gentleman who ran this thrift store threw in the chairs for free. They didn't match, but that was ok. After all this is New Mexico, and the chairs and other furniture can be as diverse as the people.

Christina and Elf watched the old man and Chad carry the furniture out to the Subaru, then smiled as she clutched the last dollar of the thirty she had made selling the gourd ornaments. She smiled at the fact that she still had a dollar left.

On the way out Chad spotted the pile of books with a sign that proclaimed "YOUR CHOICE 25¢"

He sat on the floor and began sorting through them. Several had photos of New Mexico scenery and one was all about New Mexico wild flowers. Another was a children's book titled "Animals of the Desert." He picked out three of them while Christina studied the "Gardening in the Desert" book that had a whole chapter on how to grow gourds. There went her last dollar.

Elf held up a little book she had found. Mommy smiled weakly and said, "Honey, I'm out of money. You'll have to put it back."

Reluctantly she placed the book *Farilitos of Christmas* by Rudolfo Anaya back on the pile of books and started for the door. The old man caught up with her just as she reached the sidewalk. He put the book in her hands, smiled, and said, "Enjoy it. It's a good story."

Once home they moved the furniture inside and Chad took a few of the vegetables out to Oliver who was waiting patiently for his new friends just outside the back door. He followed Chad like a puppy when he went to the well to get water for the house.

As they ate their first meal on their "new" table, stained and chipped, but much more stable than the card table had been, Chad lifted his coffee cup and gave a toast, "To the Martians in the attic."

"Daddy, they aren't Martians," Elf said looking a little exasperated.

It was late afternoon when the wind started and sand was blowing in the broken windows. Together they taped cardboard and plastic over these openings. Chad built a fire in the wood stove while Elf helped Christina carry more wood upstairs to the little stoves in what she was now calling the Martian Bakery. Then they set up the bed. Together they spread the sheets and an old quilt over the bed and fluffed up the pillows. Amid the howling wind and sound of sand hitting the sides of the house, they blew out the lantern and climbed into bed. They snuggled in the darkness and kept as quiet as they could, waiting for the arrival of what Christina was now calling the little people in our attic.

Chad had just dozed off when he heard Oliver braying outside their window. Then there were other sounds. Scurrying feet, giggles and even what sounded like singing. They quickly dressed and slipped out the front door.

As they braved the wind and silently walked around the house, they had the feeling that they were being followed. Finally Chad thought he could hear breathing behind him and turned around, flashlight in hand. There was Oliver plodding along with a silly, burro grin on his face. They turned the corner and saw, of all things, a sleigh and what appeared in the darkness to be dwarf reindeer beside the elevator. Oliver ambled over to the harness and waited for Chad. The upstairs window was open and the sleigh was filled with boxes and bags of assorted materials including flour, sugar, doll wigs, wooden blocks and so much more.

Oliver seemed to take great delight in walking this circle with the harness, turning the gears that squeaked and moaned. There was almost a rhythm to the noise. Christina and Chad, and even Elf began placing the boxes and bags from the sleigh onto the elevator. When the first couple boxes went through the open attic window and plopped onto the floor, three tiny faces appeared. There was a good deal of giggling, then one of the "little people" climbed onto the windowsill and waved. Oliver brayed and seemed to smile, or perhaps it was a burro laugh. Elf smiled and waved back while Chad placed more boxes and bags on the elevator.

The sleigh was emptied in a matter of minutes. Then Chad and Christina carried buckets of water and a bale of hay to the reindeer. Oliver joined in on this ungulate dinner party. There was a high pitched whistle from the window above. One of the little people was waving her hands.

Christina couldn't grasp what was being communicated.

Elf smiled and turned to Mommy, "I think she wants us to reverse the elevator." But Oliver was busy making friends with the reindeer. Chad pulled the lever at the base of this ancient machine, putting it into reverse. Then he grasped the harness and began to walk in a circle himself, with the belts and chains and gears making a whole different series of moans and groans.

Four little people rode the elevator down, smiled and waved to the others in the window. Soon bags and boxes of finished toys were riding the belt down to the sleigh. Elf was shaking hands and joining in their giggles. Christina helped them load the boxes of cookies and everything else until the sleigh was about half full. Then one of these little people removed her cap and pulled a handful of cookies from it. She smiled and in a most peculiar voice said, **"Thank you"** as she offered these to Chad, Christine and Elf.

Chad continued in the harness for several more minutes while eight more little people rode the elevator down to the sleigh. "Just like a ride at Disney World," one of them said as he jumped to the ground.

"Like the cookies?" the first of these little people spoke as she held out her hand, again offering the cookies to Christina. "This is my own recipe. Low fat and low carb. Lots of oatmeal and dried fruit, good for you and all the kids in the world too." She paused as Christina selected one and tasted it.

"Out of this world!" Christina spoke without thinking, then began giggling herself. It was at this point that she noticed that this little lady's hands had four rather than five fingers and there didn't seem to be any fingernails.

The cookie baker smiled, blinked her large eyes as she returned her cap to her blue tinted hair.

"Are you . . . Ahhhhh . . . Where are you from?" Christina asked as Chad joined this circle of most curious and very strange looking little people.

Part five

The little lady with the cookies smiled and looked down. "I'm from here," she answered with her large eyes half closed. She fumbled with her hair but could say no more.

The older man checking the mini-reindeer's harness looked for all the world like one of the Munchkins from the Wizard of Oz movie. The last two to come down the elevator were definitely living, breathing Gnomes. Sitting on the sleigh checking the reins was a little person dressed in a shiny dark green suit with a black hat. He was obviously an Irish Leprechaun. Securing the straps over the load of toys and cookies was another of these little people. Her long white hair hung down to her waist, but it was bushy white eyebrows and the hair on her arms that intrigued Christina.

"She's a Tomte, from Norway." The little cookie lady spoke with some hesitation. Then she continued, "I can't really tell you this," then she leaned closer and whispered, "but we are everywhere. Everywhere in the world there are little people."

The Leprechaun jumped down from the sleigh clutching what appeared to be an oversized photo album in both hands. He motioned to Chad and another of the little people who was standing in the doorway of the barn. This was a Gnome, a real, walking and talking Gnome. He had a red pointed hat, and white beard. In the middle of the beard was a gold ring that gave him a very humorous appearance. From the other side of the sleigh a voice in what could only be described as a Scottish brogue was heard. "Aye, an' don't forget the Brownies." The rather plump but dashing gentleman came around the corner wearing a plaid kilt and a brown jacket with a most colorful tam sitting rather rakishly on his head. From under this cap were flares of red hair to match the bright red beard.

From the sleigh itself another voice was heard. "We were here first, before the Anasazi, before the Folsum, before the people of Sandia." A slim, muscular individual with shiny black hair and a deep reddish-tan face stood on the seat of the sleigh. "The Comanche called us Nunnupi and the Cherokee knew my people as the Yumi. To the Shoshone we were the Nimerigar." Brightly colored feathers adorned his hair and lined the fur covered sleeves of his jacket.

Christina recognized this fur as one of the colors that had been in the attic, the faux fur for the teddy bears. He smiled as he leaped from the seat to the ground. "We are known to all the tribal people as a friend and protector of their children. My people were shy and lived in the forests and corn fields."

The Scottish Brownie motioned for everyone to sit on the sandy ground while the Leprechaun opened the large album, so large that it fit across three laps. Elf sat down right beside this strange individual and gave him a great big smile. There was constant chatter in such a variety of pitches, tones and accents.

Chad was in total disbelief. Nothing at UNM had prepared him for this. Still, he joined the circle, seating himself between a Gnome and the Nunnupi.

They all began talking and laughing at once and together, they began reciting a poem. Their diverse voices were so lyrical that it was almost a song.

Little people, Lilliputians from Jonathan Swift's sharp mind,
In the remote Buian Kara Ula Mountains of China, us you'll find.
Little people, everywhere, even the grocery store has Snap, Crackle and Pop,
Hawaii has their shy Menehune, so happy with their crafts they cannot stop.
Littlest people are the Zulu friends, the Abatwa,
who ride their ants through jungles of grass,
Hairy black Indonesian Orang-Pendeks watch over all
Who under their trees will pass.
Little people, in South America are called Duendes, but they look like a Smurf,
Pixies and Gremlins, Fairies and Trolls, all protect the peaceful people's turf.
Little people, in Russia, the Domovoi, an empty chair is set for them
beside the hearth so warm.
They maintain peace and order, but winter finds them
at wild parties, celebrating in rare form.

Little people, the Tomte, the Nisse are the protectors of every Norwegian child,
and Swedish too.
In Denmark they bring gifts and clean the house, and bake the finest cookies
and sweet treats too.
Little people watch, whoever you are, wherever you are,
wherever you go, whatever you do,
We are behind the trees, hiding in the walls, guarding your animal friends
and watching over you.

As the poem was recited, amid the giggles and laughter, Elf helped the Brownie and the Leprechaun turned the pages of the huge photo album. There were photos of each of the little people mentioned in the poem. Since these little people who occupied their attic were about the same size as Elf, she was very comfortable with them. Even when they spoke with strange accents, she seemed to be able to understand. She laughed at their jokes and simply shared the happiness that surrounded them all.

Christina and Chad were also becoming comfortable with this rather unusual assortment of new found friends. They were intrigued by the diversity of little people, and the fact that they were everywhere.

The Tomte who had shared her new cookies with them stood, and in her most professorial tone explained the discovery of the *Homo floresienses* in the caves of Indonesia. These are the archeological remains of little people who had lived perhaps 12,000 years ago. Then the one who called himself a Nunnupi described the finding of the fourteen inch tall skeletal remains considered to be an adult in Wyoming. Proof of their existence was not accepted so they were still considered mythological. Everyone laughed about this.

The Leprechaun told a joke about how the big humans insisted that the wee folk guarded a pot of gold. "The pot is really full of gold alright," he was now laughing, "but it's the golden flowers of dandelions. When we add some water and cream to these flowers they make a delicious soup. What good are gold coins? We can't eat them."

Elf was the one brave enough to ask the question her parents wanted to ask. "Why are you guys in our house?" she asked with the innocence of childhood. "I know you are all elves. But I thought you lived at the North Pole, with Santa Claus."

The oldest looking Gnome stepped forward, stroked his beard for a moment, then smiled. "It's cold up there. Our noses turn blue." He said this with a smile that implied that this was at best a half truth.

The Munchkin laughed, "You gotta tell them the whole truth. I think the little one deserves an answer. Besides, the big guys have carried wood for us and even rigged up this contraption to make our work a lot easier. We gotta tell 'em now."

"But what if they can't keep it a secret?" The Troll asked, looking doubtful.

"Sometimes we just have to trust people," the Tomte replied, passing around more of her low carb, low fat cookies. "By the way, let me know what you think of these. I'm a cookie inventor and this is my newest recipe."

The big eyed, four fingered little person stepped forward, into the middle of the circle. She cleared her throat and began. "Christmas is a season, celebrated all over the world, by many cultures, in many ways. It is the festival of the children, it is the time we rejoice in the birth of the Son of God, and the creation of all life. It is the festival of lights and that includes the lightness in our hearts when we live in the peace we all long for, even if it is for just a few days." She paused to collect her thoughts.

Then the Brownie stepped in. "In so many cultures it is a part of the tradition to give gifts and then Santa came along and expanded this idea. But there are far too many children to deliver their gifts all over the world from the North Pole in one night. Besides, all the material would have to be hauled up there. That's quite a job for these little reindeer."

Elf stood up and smiled, "I think I understand. Santa lives at the North Pole, but there are branch offices all over the world. And this is one of them." She paused, studying their faces. "Right?"

The little lady with the big eyes smiled broadly and raised her four fingered hand. "Yes, and the little people everywhere are all working together to make this a happy world for all children, and all of those willing to share the joy, the hope and the peace that lives in children everywhere."

Chad had to ask the next question. He had an idea and he just had to know if he was right. "So, the flying saucer that crashed here in 1947. Was that one of Santa's sleighs? Were the Martians really Santa's elves?"

They all laughed as the Lady with the big eyes again raised her four fingered hand, "Yes, you have guessed it. But please, keep our secret. For the sake of children everywhere, please keep our secret. But also keep the secret about the flying saucer. Your air force knows, but it has been declared Top Secret because if this information got out it could destroy Christmas for everyone."

Elf crossed her heart and sealed her lips with her fingers. "Your secret is safe with us. I promise."

They shared the rest of the cookies and then all of the little people climbed into the sleigh and the reindeer took off.

So, there you have it. Elf has asked to make you promise to keep the secret. A sleigh crashed in the desert in 1947. The Air Force helped to gather the scattered parts and even took the three little people to their hospital to heal their wounds. All three survived and are now Senior Santa Supervisors still working in distant toy factories and cookie bakeries in other remote corners of the world.

They did ask me to do one more thing for them. They all wanted me to tell you to have a peace filled holiday season, by whatever name you call it.

And on Christmas morning when you open the gifts, please whisper a few kind words for the elves. They really are everywhere. They will hear you, and it will make them smile.

In A Hurry Hawk

Growing up is hard work. It seems that some children can't wait to learn the life lessons, and are always in a hurry. A long time ago a young boy, named Little Hawk by the Medicine man, was one of those in a hurry. This is the story of Little Hawk's adventures on a trip to Grandmother's house one Christmas Eve. Little Hawk hopes you take your time and enjoy his story.

Hawk was a young boy with a quick mind, and could speak the language of the elders. He could dance the dances, even though he was a small child. He even made his own flute, and he would go to practice almost every day deep in the Canyon of the Big Rocks. Sadly, he spoke too fast and miss-spoke many of the words. He could dance well, but he was too impatient to practice. When he went to the canyon to practice his flute, he didn't take the time to listen to the voices of the canyon, the echoes. Everyone laughed and called him "Little In A Hurry Hawk."

When Auntie Nora took him to gather pinon nuts, he didn't take the time to sort the good ones from those left over from last year, or were empty. Auntie Nora watched him and shook her head. "This is why they call him Little In A Hurry Hawk," she said to the pinon trees.

Uncle Milo tried to teach him how to prepare the ground and plant the corn. But Hawk was too impatient and began planting the seeds before Uncle had thanked the Great Mystery for the sunshine and the rain, for the seeds and the wisdom of the farmer. He watched as the boy planted some seeds too deep, and failed to cover others as he hurried to get the end of the row. "Little In A Hurry Hawk is well named," Uncle said to himself.

Father took him hunting, but he wouldn't wait until the rabbit came closer and his arrows never brought anything to the stew pot. Even when they went out to harvest the spinach and wild onions from the hillside, he wouldn't take the time to thank the Great Mystery for the gift of food, and thank the plants for sharing their roots and leaves.

"Little In A Hurry Hawk has much to learn," Father said to the Great Mystery.

Mother tried to teach him how to make bread, but he wouldn't take the time to knead the dough well, so his bread was coarse and lumpy. He wouldn't wait for the oven to be warm enough to bake the bread, nor would he wait until it was done to pull the loaves from the warm horno oven. "I wish he wasn't always in such a hurry," Mother told her sisters.

Even at dinner, he wouldn't wait until everyone was served the stew before he began to eat, and he was always the first one to empty his bowl.

Hawk was impatient, so impatient that he worried his family. He worried them so much that they went to the elders and the medicine man. They talked long into the night about what to do with the boy, but after much talk they had no ideas that would work.

One of the elders suggested they tie a rock to one of Hawk's legs to keep him from running, but it was agreed that running wasn't a problem, in a hurry was.

Another of the wise old men said "If we put a big hole in his spoon, then he will have to eat slower," but everyone agreed that he would just drink his stew from the bowl and pick up the meat and vegetables with his fingers.

Finally they went home to sleep, without finding an answer to the problem of how to make Little In A Hurry Hawk slow down.

In the season to pick the corn, Hawk went into the field and picked so fast that he filled more baskets than anyone else, but he missed many of the ears. When he picked the beans, he left many on the vines. When he harvested the squash, he didn't look under the big leaves so there were many left in the field. Little In A Hurry Hawk always missed much of the harvest.

One day in the bitter cold of winter, just days before Christmas, Father created a beautiful necklace for Hawk's Grandmother. They decided that Hawk, because he was a fast runner, would deliver it to Grandmother. They agreed that he could make the journey to Grandmother's village in one day. Father packed the necklace carefully in a deerskin pouch while Mother packed a bag of food for Hawk to eat on his journey there and back. It was also agreed that he would leave at dawn the next morning. Hawk was so impatient that he couldn't sleep.

Finally, as the morning light was just beginning to show the black outlines of the hills and mountains, he dressed in his warmest clothes and picked up the two packages. Without a word he stepped out the door, ready to run all the way to Grandmother's house.

It was snowing when he began his journey, but he was able to run down the hill and across the stubble and stalks of the cornfield. But soon the snow was so thick that he couldn't see the mountains across the valley. Soon after the blizzard started, it was so deep he could no longer run. By the time he crossed the arroyo, he had to walk very slowly because the snow was almost up to his knees.

He had expected to run all the way to Grandmother's and arrive by midday, but now he was moving so slowly that he feared he wouldn't get there before sunset. He was getting tired and hungry. The blizzard winds let up so he could see again, but there was much snow left.

He stopped where the first of the big rocks were and opened the package of food that Mother had packed. In the pouch were some empty pinon shells and a note, "This is the food you didn't harvest because you were in a hurry." His mother didn't pack any food.

At first, he was angry. He threw the pouch into the snow and started again toward Grandmother's house. She would have food for Little In A Hurry Hawk. Now, each step was a struggle and he had to walk very slowly. He began to notice the birds sitting in the shrubs and on the sunflower heads. He found several seeds that the birds had left. Each one had to be shelled.

There was no way to hurry the eating of sunflower seeds. Because it took time, he began to talk with the birds, and they began to sing back to him, sharing their seeds and songs. They sang to him a song of thanks for the corn he had left in the field.

He sat on another rock and put his flute to his lips. Cracking the sunflower seeds, then playing the flute, then eating some more seeds, In A Hurry Hawk spent the rest of the morning with these birds. It was so much fun that he paused and thanked the Great Mystery for the gift of these bird friends and for the gift of the sunflower seeds.

Finally he went on his way, slowly walking through the snow. As more flakes fell in the afternoon sun, he could see the beautiful shapes of each flake. Sometimes, when they floated between him and Grandfather Sun, he could see all the colors of the rainbow in miniature. He had never noticed this before. He even invented a game. He would try to catch a single snowflake on his tongue.

As he walked on in the late afternoon sun, he spotted a cluster of berry bushes. The dried berries were hanging there, just waiting to be eaten. As he walked toward these bushes, he spotted the rabbits sitting under the bushes and reaching up to nibble the dried and frozen fruit.

In a Hurry Hawk slowly approached. "Brother Rabbit, will you share some of your berries with me?"

The Rabbits studied him for a few minutes. Finally, the smallest one spoke, "You are the boy who left the beans and squash in the field for us. Yes, we will share our berries with you."

Together they dined on delicious frozen and dried berries. Soon the sun was going down and Hawk was not to Grandmother's house yet. He couldn't walk any faster, but he knew the way and now there was a big moon to guide him.

He heard the call of the coyote, and paused to answer in his best coyote voice. This was fun. He talked with Brother Coyote for a long time. Listening carefully to the yips and yowls, he learned the language so well that others joined in from distant hills, and far away canyons.

It was just as the sun climbed over the big hills that Hawk approached the village where Grandmother lived. He paused and thanked Grandfather Sun for the light and warmth. Then, just before he reached Grandmother's house, he paused and thanked the Great Mystery for the gift of the long journey and the lessons he had learned from the birds and the rabbits and the coyotes.

Grandmother welcomed him into her house and gave him a cup of hot tea and warm corn porridge with apples. Grandmother was surprised to watch him sip the tea slowly and savor every spoonful of the porridge. Then he sat by the fire and told her of his journey. How slowly he had to walk through the snow, how Mother had packed him the food he hadn't harvested, and how the rabbits shared their berries with him. Then he gave her the necklace Father had made for her. He spent the night and following day with Grandmother, talking, gathering firewood and playing his flute for her, a nice way to celebrate Christmas Eve.

The next morning was Christmas Day. After a good breakfast, Grandmother gave him a package of food to eat on the way home, and a bag of apples to take back as a gift to Father and Mother. As he walked back in the bright white Christmas snow, he tossed bread crumbs to the birds and gave slices of apple to his rabbit friends.

He returned home just as the sun went to sleep behind the mountain that evening. He sat at the table and slowly savored the stew his mother served. Then he took out his flute and played for Mother and Father as he sat by the fire. He spoke to them in the words of the elders, and his flute playing was so calm and beautiful that those walking past entered to see who was playing. The elders all agreed that he should never be called Little In A Hurry Hawk again.

When Hawk went to the Canyon of the Big Rocks, he would play the flute, then pause and wait for the canyon to answer with the echoes. He would sometimes sing to the canyon, and it would sing back to him. One day he tried to explain to the elders how he did this, and sang in his voice and the voice of the canyon. They were so pleased that they gave him a new name, Singing Hawk.

When he danced, he was the best dancer because he was careful to keep in step and stay with the beat of the drum.

When spring came, he sang the songs of thanks before planting the corn and beans and other crops. He would pause between the planting of each seed to thank the Great Mystery for the gift of life and food and friends. But when it came the time of harvest, he still left some corn, beans and squash in the field for his friends, the rabbits and birds.

It is the way with many of us that we are in a hurry,
we miss both the view and the vision.
We forget to thank the Great Mystery, and we don't honor the earth.
We sing to the canyon and don't let it answer us.
We eat our stew without taking the time to taste it.
This is perhaps why the Great Mystery gives us occasional deep snow,
to slow our steps so that we can taste the flavors of life itself.

Tumbleweed Christmas

The young men and women who are called to serve in wars in distant places are forever changed by what they feel, see and experience. For too many, the price of conflict is carried with them as what we now call PTSD (Post Traumatic Stress Disorder). The culture shock is even greater for Native peoples. The following is a Christmas story about how one young Navajo soldier found healing in the opportunity to express his creative self. Hope you enjoy this little story from the Viet Nam era. Hector Begay could have been any of the thousands of our soldiers returning with the effects of war changing the way their minds view the world and themselves.

Please spend a few minutes with the returning veterans of today's conflicts. Listen to their stories; it's a part of the healing process.

The Viet Nam War was past for Hector Begay. He was coming home. To be more accurate, a wounded, now disabled shell of Hector Begay was on the plane that was preparing to land at the Albuquerque airport. He had survived, and other friends had not. The survivor carries a special blend of grief and guilt.

Trish and Randy wheeled him down the ramp toward the waiting family, a dinner at the Frontier Restaurant on Central, a night at the motel, then the long ride back to Window Rock. The family watched the wheelchair approach. There was no cheer, rush to embrace, no rapid fire questions. Niece Chooli did have a big red, white & blue striped balloon, but she became quiet and shy when she saw the wheelchair, and struggled to understand what it meant.

Older brother Russell greeted Hector with a handshake and a weak smile. Russ had been there two years before. He understood the reality of war, what it does to people. He knew what tomorrow would mean for his kid brother, but today they would celebrate his life and his return home alive. Tomorrow would have to take care of itself.

Over a dinner of the Frontier's famous beef enchiladas, they spoke of sheep and coyotes, of new births and old arguments. Finally Chooli began to see beyond the wheelchair, beyond the difficulty her uncle had with his right arm, and how the fingers seemed to have forgotten how to work with each other. She pulled the small package from her coat pocket and handed it to him. "Merry Christmas," there was a pause. Then she got out of her chair and came around the table. As she gave him a big hug, she continued, "Welcome home!"

He struggled to open the small box, and finally succeeded. Inside was a beautiful silver and turquoise ring. He smiled and thanked her. Then she chose the finger that she thought would be a good fit. He held up his right hand and showed his gift to everyone. His smile was genuine, but temporary. He had nothing to give in return, nothing but a smile.

Before the dinner was over, Hector had the look of exhaustion on his face. Returning home as a wounded vet is hard work. There were so many questions he wanted to answer, but no one asked.

After helping him into Russ's pickup, they drove down Route 66. Soon the city's lights were behind them. The sky was dark with low clouds threatening more snow, but, at least he was on his way home.

Home is knowing you are in the safe and protecting arms of the sacred mountains, being in the familiar desert landscape, rather than humid jungles. He could inhale the familiar scents of the juniper, clean air, sheep and horses, wood smoke and chiles. How he had longed for Auntie Rosie's tamales and Grandmother's mutton stew. Home, in so many ways, is a matter of the heart, but it is also a matter of the stomach. At home there were feasts, meals shared, and the small talk with friends and family. In the three years he had been away, babies had been born and elders had died. His mind was desperately trying to recall names, but sometimes the talking was noise, and his mind retreated to somewhere else, a place he had invented during the war, during the long weeks in the army hospital. There was too much noise, too many people, all talking at once. There was too much movement, unfamiliar faces. He leaned back and closed his eyes, seeking safety, transporting himself to some other where.

He was there again. He could see the junipers and the sheep, the magnificent patterns of the weavings, and tumbleweeds rolling across the landscape, free to roam where the wind took them. He would sometimes try to be a tumbleweed, free of the conflict, free of the orders and commands that were hard to understand. The tumbleweed was in harmony with the wind and the sun, at peace with the universe, a part of the beauty of home.

He could now BE a tumbleweed. He could set himself free and be apart from all that surrounded him and held him captive. If he were a tumbleweed, he would be free to roam with the wind, up canyons and down arroyos, pausing to visit with a juniper or rest against a corral fence. When he tried to explain this to the people around him, the doctors said he was shell shocked. His family knew he needed the healing and cleansing. They knew how killing and death affected the warrior. To get back into harmony, so that he could be free again, he needed the cleansing ceremony. The sweat lodge would be prepared and the medicine man would come to free Hector from the burden of a war half a world away.

It was strange to him, after three years in the jungle, with the smell of fear and death hanging in the air, the perpetual adrenalin high, and the effects of whatever it was they gave him daily, pills for he had no idea what, and didn't care. He couldn't care over there. Now he was home and he still had pills, and it was difficult to care here either. It was almost like a dream, or worse yet, a part of someone else's dream.

They went to the Piggly Wiggly in Gallup, but he had to wait inside the door. The damned wheelchair wouldn't fit down the aisles. Tears formed and flowed as he watched his family disappear in the canyons of shelves and beyond a mesa of Blue Bird Flour sacks.

Suddenly, he realized he was alone. The faces of those coming in the door took on a sinister appearance. Terror overwhelmed him when he realized he was unarmed. He screamed, tried to escape from the wheelchair and fell on the hard concrete floor. When Russ rushed to help, he panicked again. The sight of the pool of blood from his nose made him dizzy. Then he was somewhere else again. He relaxed in his brother's arms. He was in the desert running with the tumbleweeds, wind at his back, safe and free.

He did not want to go back to reality, but they forced him. They helped him into his wheelchair and surrounded him with handkerchiefs and advice on how to stop the blood. He was rushed out of the store and across the parking lot to the pickup.

"It's just gonna take time to get over the war," Randy said as he handed Hector a beer. "Here, this'll help."

There was snow on the ground, and it piled up high on the tumbleweed against the fence, giving the appearance of protective walls, a snow bunker. It was quiet in the vast whiteness, dark skies actually made it gray, but to Hector it was soothing. He began imagining himself walking among the snow covered tumbleweeds, talking to them, patting them on their snow white heads. It was dark when they finally got home, but his mind was still playing with his safe and silent friends.

The next morning he struggled to get the wheelchair out the door, into the bright winter sun. In the distance he saw Chooli and her friends playing in the snow. They were over in the corner of the corral where the tumbleweeds had gathered. He smiled at the sight of these children laughing among his safe friends, the tumbleweeds.

There were several of these weeds of the desert huddled against the wood pile. He began talking softly to them, so he wouldn't startle them. They asked him about the war, what it was like to be there, what he had seen, what it was like for a Navajo to be surrounded by that much death. He answered them as best he could, but mostly, he thanked them for having the courage to speak with him about the horror of that hot, humid jungle filled with bugs and bullets.

He struggled to stack these dry skeletons of once vibrant, living tumbleweeds on top of each other to make a snowman. He was trying to use sticks to bind these tumbleweeds together, give them the strength and courage to stand up to winter's North Wind. Chooli saw him and came running to greet her uncle. She was no longer intimidated by the wheelchair, or the tears that sometimes formed in his eyes. She would tell him about what she was learning at school, about the programs she saw on Lester's TV when they visited him in Gallup.

She helped him now to give this tumbleweed friend form and life. After they secured the juniper branch backbone, she began plastering it with snow. When this "tumble-man" was finished, she rounded up three more of these despised weeds and together they made another, then another. Together they made faces for them from bits of charcoal and dried apples. After Chooli had gone, he stayed with his new friends. He laughed when his mind told him what they were thinking. They were telling him how happy they were that he had "made" three new friends today. Then he began to tell them stories of the war. There was no more laughter as they stood by him, listening attentively, giving him what he so desperately needed, someone with the courage to listen. Telling these stories set the memories free and helped him cope with the trauma from what he had seen and felt.

Christmas was not a big deal with his family, and Hector was still trying to adjust to being home, and trying to understand what was wrong with him, with home, with all that surrounded him. The winter was spent by the fireplace, wishing that someone would listen to him when he needed to share the haunting memories, and cursing the legs that refused to support him. Yet every time he tried to talk about the war, they either left or changed the subject. It was a winter without laughter. It was a winter with uncomfortable feelings he tried to escape, attempted to confront, struggled to understand. At least his three tumble-friends listened.

Then in the cycle of time, spring came and he was outdoors as much as possible. Chooli appeared one afternoon waving a brown paper bag in the air above her head. "Look what I got!" she shouted as she ran toward Hector.

When she reached him, she dumped the contents into his lap. He picked up one of the small packages with bright pictures on it. "Seeds. You got a whole bunch of seeds." He smiled broadly. "You gonna plant a garden?"

"YES!" she responded as she held each one up for him to see. "Wanna help?"

There was an awkward silence before he pointed to his legs. "I ain't gonna be much help with these." She wasn't about to give up, and soon she was struggling to push the wheelchair through the moist spring earth. He was holding a juniper branch, and as they sang a traditional song Grandma Erma had taught three generations, he would punch the soil with the stick. Then he would drop several seeds into the hole. Chooli would kneel down and gently cover them, then push him ahead one turn of the wheels on his wheelchair.

It was three hours later and they had planted the entire garden; squash, corn, lots of corn, Hopi red lima beans, chiles and cabbage. Even though they both laughed and said "YUK!" when they dropped those cabbage seeds into the holes.

He smiled at the dinner table as he told everyone about planting the garden with Chooli. As the family shared the mutton stew, they also shared his hope and anticipation. This is what he was really planting that afternoon, hope along with the seeds. There was something healing about being connected with the Mother Earth.

In the weeks that followed he learned that he could hoe from his wheelchair. As the seeds sprouted and claimed their place in the sun, his mind was less often in the jungles and more frequently in the garden.

Grandma Erma was elegant in her deep blue velvet dress and her squash blossom necklace, silver bracelets and turquoise rings. She walked beside Hector and Chooli as they proudly showed her their garden. Squash blossoms were bright orange in the morning sun. The corn was knee high and the beans were blooming white and pink, with hummingbirds darting from flower to flower. Even the cabbage was growing well.

Chooli was bending down to pull some weeds but Grandma put her hand on the little girl's shoulder. "Wait. This is one of Hector's tumble-friend's children," she spoke with a smile in her voice.

Hector remembered eating the young tumbleweeds when he followed the sheep up the hills in the spring. The flavor was good and it quenched his thirst. Grandma pulled one of the little green sprouts, a plant barely three inches tall, and, as she muttered a prayer of thanks, pinched off the roots and handed it to Chooli. "Taste this, and I will tell you a story."

As Chooli chewed the crisp green seedling, Grandma began, "When I was a young girl, as was true with many of my friends, we would eat lots of tumbleweed to . . ." and she stood tall and straight as she rubbed her hands down her sides, "keep us thin and beautiful." Then she winked at Chooli, "That is, until we got married." They all laughed.

An idea was forming in Hector's mind. "Don't pull any of these. I want to do something."

"What?" Chooli asked.

When they were back in the shade sharing some cool water, Hector explained what he wanted to do. And he asked Grandma and Chooli to help him. As the garden grew and spring turned into early summer, the news traveled fast. Family and friends were all invited to join in the celebration.

Hector was throwing a feast. But there was a strange request. Everyone was asked to bring their favorite vegetable. Early in the morning Grandma, Chooli and Hector were out in the garden with baskets and bags. Then they were out behind the corral, and finally down in the arroyo. It was a ludicrous sight, Hector in his wheelchair with bags and baskets stacked so high on his lap that you couldn't see him. Chooli and Grandma Erma were each pushing one side of the wheelchair as the sun finally set itself free of the mesa's rim.

The big black kettle was sitting over the pile of wood that would soon be a fire. While this trio sat and cleaned and trimmed bag after bag of tumbleweed sprouts, others arrived with their favorite vegetables. These were cleaned, chopped, diced, and thrown into the pot along with all that tumbleweed and enough water to make a broth. Once the veggies were in the pot, everyone sat and helped clean the rest of the tumbleweed. The conversation centered on this underappreciated plant so common to the deserts and plains.

Randy told of how at Grandfather's it was so plentiful that his lambs would eat it from birth. "And his lambs never had anemia. They always seemed healthy and strong."

Alvina told about how she had heard that the runners were given tumbleweed tea to give them endurance for the races.

Others told of how when it was fed to their horses before a race, they never lost. Tumbleweed tales flowed as the big black kettle boiled and bubbled. Then Grandma and Hector's mother dumped the platter of fresh mutton into the pot. This was to be the Welcome Home for Hector. Many returning from Viet Nam never had this community of support. The three tumble-friends still stood against the wall with charcoal eyes, and someone had given them fresh new smiles.

There was music, laughter and great joy that day as they shared the tumbleweed soup. Hector never once felt the fear, or the pain and sorrow that he had carried home with him. Everyone laughed when they complained that there wasn't enough tumbleweed growing in the garden, so they had to go all the way to the arroyo for some. Everyone agreed that Hector's invention, Tumbleweed Soup, was great. The feast continued long into the night.

Summer was long and hot. Hector had to go to the VA hospital in Albuquerque for an operation that they said would give him partial use of his legs. He returned several weeks later with both a wheelchair and crutches. Chooli and Grandma Erma had tended the garden well and they had roasted corn, dried squash, and they had filled bags with the Hopi red limas. The first of the yellow melons was ripe and they dined well. Unfortunately, being back at the VA hospital brought back the old nightmares where he was back in the jungles. It took weeks with the tumble-friends and the garden before he could walk in harmony again.

With the approach of fall, with cold winds and tumbleweeds racing across the landscape, there was a sadness to Hector's tentative steps with the crutches. There were no jobs and food was becoming scarce. The family was thankful for all the food that came from Chooli and Hector's garden. They were able to share with uncles and aunties and the elderly couple who lived up the canyon. Still, Hector felt that he was a burden to his family. The nightmares haunted his fitful sleep more frequently.

The frost glistened in the early morning sun. The flies were gone and Hector and his family were visiting some friends to help with a butchering. The fire was glowing brightly when a tumbleweed blew across the open space and rested between Hector and the flames. The tumbleweed seemed to glow with red, yellow and orange lights.

Alvin laughed, "Looks like a Christmas tree, don't it."

But Hector was already thinking. He struggled with the crutches and hobbled over to the tumbleweed pausing in its journey, perhaps to warm itself by the flames. He reached down to pick it up. It laughed at him and rolled just out of reach. He spoke to it and followed on his crutches. Each time he came close enough to grab it, that old tumbleweed would laugh, and tumble out of reach again. He chased it across the yard until it finally reached the corral fence. Trapped, it looked up at him and smiled. He gently picked it up and carried it back to the fire.

Alvin, Grandma Erma and all the others were watching and laughing at the absurd sight of Hector herding a tumbleweed.

He removed a shoe lace and threaded it through his tumbleweed mustang, then tied it to his crutch. The laughter was contagious and it continued for some time. But Hector was thinking about Christmas trees. It would be so nice to have a tumbleweed Christmas tree for his tumble-friends.

As Russ helped him into the pickup, he untied the captured tumbleweed and, after becoming comfortably seated, he gently placed the tumbleweed on his lap while his brother tossed the crutches into the back. On the way home Russ kept glancing at his brother and the beautifully formed tumbleweed tethered by a shoelace. He finally spoke up, "What ya ought to do is paint it."

Hector was trying to imagine how you could paint such a complex structure as this, when Russ began fumbling under the seat as they bounced along the unpaved road. Finally he held up a can of bright blue spray paint. They both laughed at the thought of a blue Christmas Tumble-tree.

It was in the first light of a clear cold October morning when Hector leaned against the post beside his tumble-friends, explaining what he was doing with the paint and the tumbleweed hanging from his shoelace. They smiled but didn't answer, until he placed it against the wall beside them. Then they looked to the north and spoke to him about the wind and what would happen to their tumble-tree.

He found a couple pieces of sandstone and anchored it in place. Then he went inside to put more wood on the fire and refill the coffee pot.

It was later in the morning when Grandma Erma came into the yard. She parked the old black pickup by the outhouse. As she reached the door, she saw the bright blue tumbleweed beside Hector's three tumble-friends. She smiled and walked over to the pinon tree by the sheep pens. She collected a handful of pine cones and carefully placed them, like Christmas tree ornaments, on the blue tumbleweed.

After a cup of coffee, she led Hector outside and showed him how she had decorated his tree. After school Chooli stopped by. When she saw the blue tumble-tree with pinon cone decorations, she went around the house to Auntie's rose bushes. There she collected a handful of bright red rose hips. These she tied into clusters with green yarn. Then she tied them onto the tumbleweed.

Hector was again led out the door to see his tumble-tree. Chooli was so proud of her ornaments. They were standing in the late afternoon sun when Uncle Ernie drove into the yard. He laughed loud and long when he saw what they had created. Then without a word, he returned to his truck and, after several minutes rummaging through a burlap bag, he rejoined them. He had four small gourds that he hung around the blue painted tumbleweed.

"You can paint these and bet they'd sell in Albuquerque. Them crazy Anglo tourists, they'll buy anything." He said smiling at the tumble-tree. "I bet you can even sell tumbleweeds if you trim 'em up like that."

In the days that followed, while the wind swirled around the house and the first real snow of the season fell for a short visit, Hector, Chooli and Grandma sat around the table painting gourds, tying decorations made from dried flowers dipped in dyes, even attaching small bunches of tiny red chiles.

Hector had collected about a dozen tumbleweeds, now stacked against the wall by his bed. It became a Navajo joke that spread faster than the wind. "Hector is making Christmas trees out of tumbleweeds. He thinks he can sell 'em in Albuquerque. That war did something to his mind."

When the word got out that after only one more tumbleweed he was out of spray paint and had no money to buy more, folks started dropping by to see just how he turned a tumbleweed into a Christmas tree. Of course, when they visited, they always had a can of spray paint they had left over from some project. A few even stopped in after they had to run into Grants for something. They saw that spray paint was on sale at Kmart and picked up a can for him.

Most afternoons you would find Hector over in the lean-to shelter by the sheep pens with tumbleweeds hanging from the rafters, spray can in hand. He had a rainbow of tumble-trees; red, green, blue, white, pink, and purple. Even the ornaments were becoming colorful after Doc. Salazar stopped by to check on Hector's legs and left off two cans of gold and silver paint. When Russ asked what he thought the tumbleweeds would sell for, Doc rubbed his chin, then his moustache before answering. He didn't want to give any false hope. Still, it was Christmas season. Finally, he gave a cautious answer, "I'd guess maybe as much as two, maybe three dollars each."

On Nov. 3rd Hector had to go back to the VA hospital. He carefully placed two of his best tumble-trees in bushel baskets while Grandma and Chooli carefully wrapped gourds, gold and silver pine cones, dried flower ornaments and mini chile ristras.

It was late in the afternoon when the doctors were finished poking and prodding Hector's legs and telling him to walk more. They got to Old Town at just a little past four. Hector wanted to go to the Basket Shop, but Russ suggested that the Gallery might pay more. Hector hobbled into the bright white room with paintings on the walls and sculptures on the tables and display stands. The old man in the black suit was thanking the clerk for her service as he carefully placed a small package in his briefcase. He saw them entering and watched as Hector took his favorite tumble-tree from the basket and sat it on the counter. It was sprayed green inside and the tips of each branch were white. On top was a silver painted pinon cone and around the sides were four other ornaments, samples of what Grandma and Chooli had done.

"What is this?" the man in the black suit asked as he walked around the strange looking object. "What a splendid example of Environmental Art, with the most ubiquitous of weeds as the medium." He looked around the shop and when certain the clerk was busy with another customer, motioned for them to follow him outside. Then he whispered, "What are you asking for this exquisite work?" he asked.

Hector was ready to answer, "three dollars," but the old man didn't give him a chance to speak. "I'll give you one-fifty, not a penny more."

Hector was crushed. He had hoped to get at least two dollars each from these tumbleweed trees. "I-I-I was h-h-hoping for t-t-two," he finally stuttered.

"All right. I've got to have it. Two it is." He said as he took his wallet from his pocket and removed two crisp one hundred dollar bills.

Hector gasped, and started to say "I meant two dollars," but Russ stepped between them and grabbed the cash as he interrupted his brother. "You realize you just got quite a bargain here, but he's a Nam Vet. Needs the money bad. For surgery on his legs."

"I've got to hurry. Don't want to miss my train back to Phili." He spoke fast, as he took a card from his pocket, "Would you write your name on this so I can get top dollar for it as a signed work of art in my gallery, Art on the Horizon, in Philadelphia?"

Hector took his pen and scribbled his name on the back of the card.

"Now, would you be so kind as to give me your address, so that we can negotiate future purchases?"

As he turned and walked toward the church clutching the tumble-tree in the bushel basket, the clerk was completing her sale. Hector turned the other way and walked to their parked truck where he retrieved the second tree. As he reentered the gallery, Russ and the clerk were unwrapping the ornaments. She smiled as he approached and asked, "Navajo hand-crafted ornaments, made from Nature?" But she didn't wait for a response. She gasped when Hector pulled the pink and pale blue tumble-tree from the basket. "Wait right here!" she spoke in hushed tones as she turned and almost ran into the back room. In less than a minute a tall, rather stern looking woman with a Navajo turquoise and silver necklace and silver combs in her gray hair came over to them.

She spoke not a word as she examined the tumble-tree in Hector's hands. Finally she responded with only a "Hmmmmmmmmmmmmmmmm," before turning her attention to the ornaments Russ was now spreading out on the counter. She gently picked up one after another, holding it up to the light, then against the tumbleweed. "I've never seen anything like this," she finally spoke as she arranged and rearranged the ornaments.

She studied Hector, the way he had to lean against the counter, the cane that he was now walking with. "War Vet?" she asked with a look of intense sadness in her eyes.

Hector nodded and started to speak, but she interrupted him. "I lost a son in that horrid war. He wasn't twenty yet. About your age, I'd guess." Her sorrow quickly turned to anger, "Why would they send our finest children, children of the desert, to fight a war in a jungle? How serious are your injuries?"

Hector started to explain about his legs and how badly the nerves and muscles had been damaged, while she wiped the tears from her eyes. "Constance tells me that you sold one of these to Gordon Stuart of Art on the Horizon. Could I ask how much he paid you?"

After a brief discussion about Mr. Stuart's gallery and the benefits of dealing locally, she asked one more question. "How soon can you deliver six more of these, what did you call them?"

Hector liked this elderly Anglo lady. In so many ways she reminded him of Grandmother Erma. "I have eight more done. Each is a different color. In fact," and he started to laugh, "No two are the same because I have to use half empty cans of paint from friends. Can't afford to buy any myself."

For the first time in the conversation the old lady smiled. "Oh, I wouldn't want any two to be the same, but I would want each one signed."

She matched Gordon's offer and added $500.00 for the box of handcrafted Environmental Art ornaments. It was also agreed that they would deliver the rest of the tumble-trees and at least four dozen ornaments before the end of the week.

Hector didn't recall ever having that much cash in his hands. They stopped at the Piggly Wiggly on the way back to the rez. This time he was loading carts full of almost everything he could imagine his family needing for the rest of the winter. There was no apprehension about who might be lying in the next aisle. He bought $300.00 worth of food for the family, the extended family and neighbors. The bed of the old pickup was almost full of grocery bags. Then they stopped at the hardware store and bought ten cans of spray paint. Finally they pulled into the thrift store and bought a good warm winter coat for everyone he could think of. While they drove out Route 66, Hector counted the money he had left. He had six dollars and 56 cents. But he felt good about himself, better than he had for at least three years. He was happy, happy because of a bunch of silly old tumbleweeds. Happy because he had become an artist, a person with a creative identity.

He leaned back and slept for more than two hours of the ride home. Two hours of sleep without images of the jungle, smells of fear and death, the sound of planes and gunfire, the taste of food without chile. He dreamed of sheep safely grazing under a star filled sky. He dreamed of peace.

It was truly a Tumbleweed Christmas.

The tumbleweed, though much cursed and despised, has become a part of the landscape and traditions of the West. So many tumbleweed tales have been shared with us, delightful stories, some true, others creative. We welcome your recollections of encounters with or uses for this, the ultimate weed of the West. Since the raw materials are readily available, you might want to be as creative as Hector Begay and design a tumble-tree for yourself.

All I Want for Christmas Is a Unicorn

Perhaps by sharing this story, other children will be freed to share their stories, their feelings, their loneliness, their fear, and their hope. Perhaps they too will want a unicorn for Christmas. May you have a Merry Christmas, and let us all pray for Peace Beyond All Fear, for all the children of the world.

Denise was waiting for the nurse to come and take her into the other room where they would give her the chemotherapy treatments. She remembered when she began to feel weak, and the look on Mommy and Daddy's faces when the doctor told her parents she had leukemia. The doctors talked to her parents using words she didn't understand. Nurses took blood from her arm, and they gave her pills that helped make the pain go away. Now she was spending two weeks at the Children's Hospital in Albuquerque. They were giving her chemicals that would fight this cancer that made her hurt and made Mommy & Daddy look so sad. She was scared. She didn't like being at the Children's Hospital and wanted to get better so she could go home.

With her in this waiting room were eleven other children. There was some whispering and a few of the children were busy coloring or playing the game that was in the little book the lady at the desk had given them with a smile and a "Merry Christmas." Others were simply sitting, very still, quiet and scared.

Each of them had strings of beads, different colors and shapes. Each time they came down for a chemotherapy treatment, they got another string of beads from the desk lady. Denise now had seven. Paul had so many he couldn't count them all. Elina was now wearing her first one.

Suddenly the door swung wide open and Nurse Hadley entered pushing a wheelchair. Everyone laughed. Riding in the rainbow painted wheelchair was about the biggest teddy bear they had ever seen. He was wearing a Santa hat and a bright red nose, and he was hugging a story book.

Everyone laughed when Nurse Hadley and the bear began singing "Rudolph the Red Nosed Reindeer." Soon everyone, even the parents joined in. At the end of the song, that silly ole bear's nose began to glow brightly. That was the name the children gave him that day, Ole Bear.

While they waited for the doctor to arrive, Ole Bear leaned back in the rainbow wheelchair and opened the book. He read them the story about a sad little teddy bear who was in a hospital and was sad, and lonely, and scared. This was until she was visited by an invisible unicorn.

The little teddy bear in the story seemed to Denise to be a lot like herself. They were both bald, and they both wore caps knitted by their mommies. And they both had needles where the medicine in the bag was put into them to fight the cancer. Just like the little teddy bear, she was scared. She didn't know what a unicorn was, but she wanted one, too.

The Ole Bear held up the book for all the children to see. It was a picture of a pony with a horn in the middle of its forehead. It was standing beside the hospital bed where the little teddy bear was reaching out to give it a great big hug.

Denise raised her hand, "Are there really unicorns?"

Ole Bear closed the book and leaned forward. "OHHH YES! Unicorns have been around for a long, long time. Some call them mythical beasts, but I think they're super heroes."

"Wow, do they fight bad guys?" Paul asked.

The big bear laughed, "The unicorn is a wonderful creature who fights fear, and loneliness and sadness, not with fists, or guns, or swords. No, the unicorn uses more powerful weapons than those. Unicorns fight fear with love, loneliness with smiles, and sadness with hope."

"WOW!" Denise said as she touched the IV port on her arm. "Wish I had a unicorn." Then she lowered her head, "Cancer is scary, and the needles hurt." She muttered.

That's where it all started.

One at a time the children were taken from the waiting room into the treatment room. Nurse Hadley and Ole Bear sat and chatted with the children about Christmas and other winter holidays, and colored pictures along with them in the little activity books. Ole Bear, with his big paws, wasn't really good at coloring, but he tried anyway. They even sang a couple more songs.

Denise was drawing something on her tablet and Ole Bear leaned forward to see what she was doing. "Beautiful!" he exclaimed as held up her drawing for all to see. It was a blue unicorn, complete with a horn in the middle of its forehead and a bright yellow necklace that said H-O-P-E in big white letters.

Everyone, even nurse Hadley, clapped their hands when they saw her picture.

"All I want for Christmas is a unicorn," she said shyly, "Just like this one."

One by one they were taken into the treatment room. Nurse Hadley and Ole Bear formed a circle with the rest of the children and their parents. Ole Bear took a red light bulb from his pocket and held it up for all of them to see. Suddenly it lit up and glowed brightly. Next he held up a green light bulb in his left hand. When it began to glow too, everyone clapped.

Ole Bear told them, "This is the season of lights," he pointed to the menorah with the Hanukkah candles sitting on the desk, then to a picture of a great bonfire and people dancing around it, then he asked if any of them had ever seen the Northern Lights. "All over the world, during the darkest days of the year, the earth and all its people celebrate with lights." Then his red nose glowed brightly again and everyone laughed. For a moment everyone forgot about cancer, and the fear, and sadness and just laughed. All except Elina.

She was starting to cry. This was her first treatment, and she didn't know what to expect.

Denise handed her unicorn picture to Elina and patted her hand. "You can have my unicorn. It will keep you from being afraid while you are in the treatment room."

Elina tried to smile as she muttered "Thank you," but the tears continued to flow.

Ole Bear handed her his silk handkerchief from his pocket. Even Elina had to laugh as, one after another, colorful handkerchiefs were pulled from his pocket.

"The chemo will help you get better," Denise said. Then she quietly paused. "I hope," she added, almost whispering.

One by one the children left the waiting room for their treatment sessions. Then it was Denise's turn. She had been through this six times, but she was still scared, still lonely and still not really hopeful. She waved to Ole Bear and Nurse Hadley as she was wheeled through the door.

Denise was very tired after the treatment session and was asleep before she got back to her room. The nurse gently placed her in bed and tucked the covers around her.

Denise opened her eyes and smiled as she saw the little Christmas tree in the corner. The nurse said, "Yes. It's almost Christmas. What do you want Santa to bring you?"

"A unicorn, a real live unicorn, just like in the story." Denise answered, "All I want for Christmas is a unicorn." And her eyes closed again for a long afternoon nap. Mommy & Daddy kissed her on the forehead and tip-toed from the room.

From that day on, every time someone visited her, they brought a little unicorn and placed it on her tree. Some brought her a unicorn picture that they hung on the wall. One of her aunts gave her a pillow with a unicorn on it. She had so many unicorns, she shared them with her friends and all the other cancer patients in the Children's Hospital. Nurse Hadley started calling her "The Unicorn Kid."

But she was still scared, still lonely and still not very hopeful. It was Christmas Eve and Mommy and Daddy spent the whole evening with her in her hospital room. Mommy had baked some of her special Gingerbread people and Denise and the other children in the room helped decorate them with icing and colored sugar. Daddy told the Christmas story and they all sang Christmas carols. Denise was now very tired, and so were the other children in the hospital. One by one they fell asleep, and so did Denise. The parents all left and the lights were turned out.

In the darkness Denise thought she heard a noise and opened her eyes. There standing beside her bed was the most beautiful creature she had even seen. It was pure white except for a pale blue mane and a most delicately spiraled golden yellow horn. A small hoof tapped her blanket and she sat up. When she patted the unicorn's mane, it was as soft as velvet. It was such a gentle creature, yet strong. YES! This was her super hero. There was even a bright yellow bead necklace around its neck with white letters that spelled H-O-P-E.

She gathered all the unicorn ornaments from her little Christmas tree and climbed on his back.

Together they went from room to room, and on each pillow she placed one of her ornaments. With the unicorn's help she was giving each child the courage of love, the comfort of a smile and hope found in friendship.

They came to the last room in the hall, Elina's room, but she was out of unicorn ornaments. This mythical beast lowered his head, and the yellow necklace fell onto Elina's pillow.

Denise awoke as the first rays of sun were shining through the window, making all the unicorn ornaments on her tree glow. She smiled as she remembered who had given her each of them. Then she remembered her ride on the blue unicorn, delivering those ornaments to all the other children. "It must have been a dream," she whispered to herself. The nurse came into the room and took her temperature and blood pressure. She was taken down to the garden room where the big Christmas tree was. Parents and family filled the room and, as the children entered, they all began to sing. Even Ole Bear was there with his silly red glowing nose.

Elina was the last of the children to enter the garden room. She was smiling. She was also wearing a bright yellow bead necklace with white letters that spelled H-O-P-E.

A unicorn may be the super hero in this little story, but the real super heroes are all the children, their families and friends and all those who work in the children's hospitals who, like the unicorns, fight fear with love, loneliness with smiles and sadness with hope.

Betting on the Quilt

Being a teenager is not easy. There is that ill-defined matter of self-image, pride, and the very difficult challenge of finding yourself. Every step of the way there is someone just waiting to tell you that you are wrong, not good enough, stupid, weak, a failure. Your mistakes are circled in red on the schoolwork, parents scold you because you don't think the same way an adult does, and your peers mock you when you don't make the same bad choices they do. But sometimes, when given the opportunity and encouragement, teens are capable of being heroes in their own special way. Wrap up in a nice warm quilt and enjoy this little story.

Part one

"You want me to do what?" Nadine rose from her chair and pointed her finger at the principal. "No way! No how! Not me! Not on your life!"

Ms. Albright, the Juniper Crossing High School principal, smiled that benign smile of hers, but this time it didn't seem to be disarming her art teacher. "But, look at this as an opportunity to make a real difference." The smile broadened and she added, "Besides, I bet real money on you doing this. Think about it. You keep these boys out of jail for the rest of the school year, and the art department gets the gift of $1,000 for each one of them who completes this project for Judge Marvin Melchior."

Nadine sat down and put her hands on the table. "Let me get this straight. You want me to teach seven teenage boys how to make a quilt?"

Ms. Albright knew she was now winning. She leaned back and closed her eyes. She could see the money, $7,000 in dollar bills covering the floor and the desks in the art room. The smile broadened as she envisioned the materials that this money could bring into a class that the school

99

board wanted to discontinue. She understood very well the passion with which Nadine Alvarez approached her art, and her students. It was this ability to read people, draw out their talents and answer their needs that had made MS. Albright a successful teacher and now a most unique high school principal.

Juniper Crossing High School was not located in an affluent community. It had more than its fair share of at risk youth, troubled teens, students with learning disabilities, and now a gang that had tagged the property of another school. The student body was a patchwork quilt of colors, nationalities and languages. Perhaps that's where the problem began, but somehow, deep inside that caring mind of hers, she knew this diversity was also the strength of this community. These boys were survivors, all they needed was a sense of direction, a goal that used their diverse talents, their agile hands and strong bodies.

It all began with the first football game of the season when a group of students from Carlton HS made a couple of insulting comments about the Juniper Crossing team of mongrels. It degenerated into name calling and some racial slurs, then a fist fight. Incidentally, the Juniper Crossing Coyotes won, but that caused even more problems. They sought revenge when the Carlton boys hung the stuffed coyote that served as the school mascot from the cottonwood at the entrance to the school parking lot. These seven wayward teens broke into the gym at Carlton and painted coyotes on a number of the Carlton players' uniforms. Then they spray painted rather crude comments on the windows of the rival school. In all honesty, their art work was superior and that's what gave the good judge the idea that the principal was now trying so hard to sell.

They were, of course, captured on the security cameras and ended up at the police station the next afternoon. Chaco was a large Navajo, not a good student because he needed to be doing something with his hands, but he was a natural born leader. Dwight was Anglo. His mother ran the convenience store in Juniper Crossing. Tan was Chinese and Laguna mix, tall and lean with thick glasses and an attitude. Streak was an African-American who earned his nickname by streaking naked across the football field during a game two years ago. He was both a hero to the student body and a serious concern to the faculty. Rico was Hispanic and he carried an anger just below the surface that made everyone cautious. Cowboy was really an Indian. His father was Lakota and his mother was Apache. He was one of the few kids in the school who owned his own horse. He had to repeat almost every class in both 9th and 10th grade, but had a wall full of trophies from the local rodeos and fairs.

The last member of this "gang" was known as Juarez. It was unclear whether or not he was an illegal alien. There were always questions about his papers. He spoke little, but did possess the ability to cuss in English and Spanish, and all too often he utilized this talent to insult the teachers and embarrass his female classmates.

Because each of these kids had problems, they were considered problems themselves. Broken homes, alcoholic parents, AWOL dads, poverty, lack of educational basics, short emotional fuses and other factors made these seven who they were. When Ms. Albright came to the school in August she was warned about each of them. Now she understood why many of the faculty members were so hard on them, and why the rest were afraid of them. When they united they were a force to be reckoned with.

When the date of their hearing arrived, Juniper Crossing High School principal, Dale E. Albright, asked to speak to the judge. She had read about his interest in horse races and had seen him at the casino numerous times. She knew how to handle a gambler, after all she was one herself. She gambled with life. That was what had made her such a good English teacher, and now a damn good principal. It occasionally got her into trouble, too.

Her comment, made behind the solid pine doors of Judge Melchior's chambers, was the plea of a teacher, a surrogate parent, an old lady who loved all of her children and wanted to keep them safe. She knew that suspension was not the answer, nor was time in juvenile detention. This would make them all negative heroes.

She pleaded for their futures, "Your Honor, I bet you I can turn these boys around and avoid the curse of juvenile detention, which as you and I both know is nothing more than a graduate course in crime." She spoke with passion. Unfortunately, as was often the case with Ms. Albright, she spoke before thinking through just what it was she was saying.

The aging judge watched her eyes. This was a petite old lady with gray hair in braids and wearing strings of beads, love beads left over from the Sixties, but there was an intensity in her eyes. He could envision her as a student at UNM in those days of protest and progress. Those were the days when it all seemed to be within their grasp. Not money, fortune and the accumulation of stuff and nonsense. No, what the people like this lady were reaching out for was the stuff that counted; peace and justice, the equality of all men and women, the freedom of everyone to live in harmony and follow the dove of peace over the rainbow and into the Age of Aquarius.

He knew this because he too had been one of these peaceniks, he also had bell bottom blue jeans and love beads that were the outward expression of the vision within. He knew all the songs she would have sung, the joy she would have known as she marched for peace in front of the Student Union Building, picketed the Roundhouse in Santa Fe for equal pay for equal work, and volunteered with the health services on the reservations, tutored in Albuquerque's barrios and drank the sweet wine of youth.

"The public demands that they be punished," he said, almost apologetically. He removed his glasses and leaned forward. "What do you think would be an appropriate punishment?" He then smiled at his own cleverness. The burden had been moved to her aging shoulders. He wanted to see how she would respond. He hoped for a creative solution and was ready to weigh her thoughts.

"Your Honor, these kids are a patchwork quilt of our youth, they wanted to avenge a wrong, and they united together for their own support because the community wasn't about to give them what they need. They need support, not punishment. What if we give them a community service project with a positive goal; something that lets them work together and be a positive example for the rest of our students? Let's take a chance on these kids. I'm willing to bet you they can work together to accomplish something good."

"A patchwork quilt of our youth. Yes, that's it." The judge leaned back, a victorious smile spreading across his face. "Let's have them make a quilt. Think these wayward youths can make quilts?" The smile became almost a laugh as he closed his eyes and gave his mind the freedom to envision the product of its creative imagination.

Mrs. Albright, rarely at a loss for words, was now searching for a response. This wasn't what she envisioned. She smiled at the image of these wayward youths gathered around the table, a different kind of needle in hand. The Quilting Bee Gang perhaps? She also envisioned the challenge this would present. How could she possibly talk them into this?

"Don't think you can get them to do it?" he teased.

She blurted it out before thinking it through. "I'll bet you a year's worth of art supplies my boys can, and will make a quilt. What's more, I'll bet you it's a work of art when they are done with it." Now the smile was on her face.

He laughed out loud, and leaned forward. "You're on!" Now he wanted to make this bet a little more interesting. "I'll help you out," he said. "I'll give your art department $1,000 out of my own pocket for each one of these seven boys who sees this project through to the end. But if they fail to produce a quilt, then we can forget about an art department at Juniper Crossing High School."

He had called her bluff, but she was already thinking of ways to motivate these seven troubled teens. An idea was beginning to take shape in her mind as they shook hands to seal the bet.

It was a far more difficult challenge for the judge to sell this idea to the folks at Carlton High. They wanted hard labor with a diet of bread and water. The hearing was postponed until January 15th. It was also agreed that the boys would bring their quilt into the good judge's chambers before Christmas. If they actually presented a completed quilt, he would have the cash ready for the art teacher. Judge Melchior hoped that these boys would succeed, even if it cost him $7,000. He had almost made up his mind to give the school the money even if the boys failed. Money is only as good as what you can do with it.

Part two: Nadine to the Rescue

That was what brought Nadine to the principal's office this Friday afternoon, a gambling bet between a judge and a high school principal. Nadine was intrigued by the stakes in this bet. She too could envision what $7,000 would do for her meager art department, and her own bank account, because most of the supplies now used were bought with her own money and a few donations from the local craft store.

They outnumbered her seven to one, but that made it just about an even match. She had put a good deal of thought into how this could work, how she could make it work. First she wanted to keep them together. She understood that they were support for each other when the rest of the world seemed to be against them. These boys were a family of choice because their biological families had failed them. The community, the school, the other students all too often viewed them as failures, and didn't hesitate to tell them that was all they would ever be, failures and troublemakers. She understood very well that kids will either live up to or down to the expectations of their elders and peers.

"Please be seated," she spoke with that soft voice and benign smile of hers as she made eye contact with each one of them. "We have an opportunity here to do something that's never been done in the history of Juniper Crossing High School."

This isn't what they had expected. Suspension, jail time, failure and punishment were at the forefront of these young minds. They were still suspicious, but the defensive and sullen attitudes were being replaced with a good measure of curiosity.

Chaco spoke first, "What you got up your sleeve?" He still felt uncomfortable sitting there on those hard, scarred and uncomfortable chairs. He was waiting for the condemnation, the lecture, the threats that always marked a visit to the principal's office.

This was the opening she needed. "The future of the art department depends on you gentlemen."

"Bullshit?" they responded almost in unison.

Ms. Albright noted their expressions. Chaco wouldn't admit it but he was, in his own way, an artist. He almost smiled at the thought that he could do something that would finally make his grandmother proud. Streak immediately saw this as a way to impress Carlota, whom he viewed as a work of art, although she thought of him as little more than a nuisance. Tan was the only one with his lips tightly locked in a frown. Cowboy was rubbing his chin envisioning the kind of art he could paint on the side of the Carlton gym. Dwight was the only one without an expression. He was always the most difficult student in the whole school to read. Rico had an incurable habit of sketching all sorts of skulls in his textbooks, and Juarez was too intimidated to voice an opinion in this office.

"It's also a way to beat that Carlton bunch and be real heroes in Juniper Crossing." Her voice sounded conspiratorial as she continued to tease them without coming out and telling them they had to make a quilt. It was becoming clear to these boys that this principal might be on their side, even though it didn't dawn on a single one of them that they were on her side. Within five minutes she had a team dedicated to winning, even if they didn't know what the game was yet.

"They wanted to lock you boys up for a couple months, but we came up with a better idea," she was confiding now and her voice became almost a conspiratorial whisper. "I bet $7,000 worth of art supplies, that you boys can make a quilt for the homeless shelter." She gave them a moment to let the words sink in, before she continued, pretty much making it up as she went along. "How do you think we can best do this?" she asked, drawing them into the planning, making this their project, if not their idea.

Rico spoke first, "A quilt? You want us to make a Goddamned quilt?"

103

Streak just started to laugh, but Chaco motioned for him to be quiet. "I know how to weave a little," he spoke with a certain pride, "Grandmother taught me when I was a little kid, but I'm better with silver and turquoise."

Ms. Albright called for Nadine to join them. While they waited for the art teacher to arrive, Ms. Albright pulled a patchwork quilt from the big box sitting on the floor. Without a word she spread it over the clutter that always covered her desk. This was a simple pattern of squares, rectangles and triangles of various sizes; each cut from bandanas. The boys surrounded the desk, examining the way the odd sized pieces were put together, studying the tight even stitches and the border of red bandana fabric.

When Nadine entered the office, the boys dropped the fabric and immediately adopted the slouch and swagger that was their trademark. Ms. Albright motioned for her and the boys to be seated and she pulled her chair from behind the desk, placing it so that she was a part of an informal circle. She had a sparkle in her eyes as she turned her attention to Nadine. "I would like to introduce your new, advanced art class."

Nadine was still unsure, but in her mind each of her students was a work of art, unique, dynamic, filled with potential and talent. She looked at each student walking these paint crumbling halls and saw a rare, valuable gemstone in the rough. It was her job to bring each of these gems into the light; clean, polish, make them shine. Right now, as she looked over this slouching and surly collection of wayward youth, it was difficult to envision much potential. Still, she would try, for the sake of the art supplies, and the continuation of her now marginalized department and teaching position. She began by firing questions at the boys. "Have you ever done any sewing?" she was looking over her reading glasses perched precariously on the tip of her nose. The response was universal. Not a single one of these boys was about to admit it, even if they had.

Ms. Albright jumped in, pointing toward Chaco, "He has some experience with silver work, and they all demonstrated a certain artistic skill over at Carlton." She was smiling as if she took a certain pride in their delinquent activity, or perhaps it was their willingness to express the creativity residing within each one of them. This, she considered an act of courage. All self-expression was an act of courage to the teens in this low end school.

Streak leaned back in his chair, studying the principal. He may have had trouble reading American Lit, but he was very good at reading people. This was a survival skill. For some strange reason, it seemed to him that she really was on their side. He laughed, then, with eyes focused on Nadine, he spoke. "You mean you want us to sew a quilt so we don't spend time in the detention center?"

Cowboy glanced at Streak, then toward Ms. Albright. He chose his words carefully. "You just don't get it, do you?" He leaned forward and continued, "Servin' time proves somethin' to the rest of the world."

Juarez seemed nervous as he fidgeted in his chair, "Yeah, but that can hurt the whole family." Then he slumped forward, refusing to look the teacher and principal in the eye. "I say we do it and get it over with."

One by one they expressed their thoughts, opinions, fears and concerns. Tan didn't want anyone to know because everyone would make fun of him. Dwight thought it might be ok, but didn't want anyone watching them while he sewed.

"No way, Man. I ain't gonna do it." Rico glared at Ms. Albright. After a pause when no one responded, he added. "I got my pride."

Nadine finally spoke up, "You guys mean something to Juniper Crossing, and to me. You're our Magnificent Seven, and you can save the art department. Isn't that proving something to the world?"

Chaco stood and took the quilt in his hands. He studied it closely again, feeling the texture, running his fingers over the stitches. Nadine noticed that his eyes were closed. He was somewhere else, but she didn't know where.

He was back in Grandmother's hogan. He was a small child. There was a fire in the little wood stove that heated the single room that was her home. He put another piece of pinon in the stove, then walked over to the spools of wool, different colors, but all made with Grandmother's aging hands, helped by his nimble fingers. Outside he could hear the rhythmic tapping of Grandfather's hammer on the silver he worked. In this journey into yesterday, the time when he was a child, he realized something. This was the work of artists. Grandmother and Grandfather were artists. Perhaps there was something of the artist within him, something just waiting to be discovered, to be set free.

He opened his eyes and smiled at the quilt. In his mind he was now seeing the pictures that were a part of his grandmother's weaving, and the flowers and leaves formed in the silver by Grandfather's hands. "Does it have to be just shapes like this, or can we make pictures?"

The others looked at him, puzzled, confused. Was he seriously considering going along with this crazy idea?

Ms. Albright started to speak, but Nadine interrupted, "I, ahh, we, would hope that you use this as an opportunity to express yourselves. Whatever form that takes."

Ms. Albright felt it was time to close the deal. "Are you guys in? Ya got guts enough to do it?"

Dwight looked to Chaco, then nodded. He would follow if Chaco was willing to lead. Tan was reluctant, frowning and refusing to look at the quilt on the desk.

Cowboy laughed again, "Can I do one of these squares with a painting of a horse on it?" He was testing them, trying to find the limits.

"As long as it isn't obscene, or offensive, you can make any designs for your quilt that you would like."

"Can we really paint on the cloth?" Streak asked, now leaning forward.

Nadine smiled, knowing that they were going to do it. These kids, her own Magnificent Seven, were going to make a quilt for the homeless shelter. They were going to get seven thousand dollars for the art department. They were on their way to becoming heroes, in a most absurd way.

Juarez smiled and spoke up, "I was just thinking. In my Mexico, we have the Tree of Life that is a part of our Christmas celebration. We could each be a branch on that tree."

The rest of the afternoon was spent with the seven youths drawing sketches for a quilt design. Dwight offered to have his mother come in and show them how to do the fine even stitches. Meanwhile, Nadine was starting to compose her shopping list of all the things she wanted to have for her art department. It was fun to plan just how far seven thousand dollars could go.

It soon became the talk of the school. Everyone was speculating on whether these seven teen-age boys would really make a quilt. Bets were being made on the probability of these seven teens, none of whom had ever taken an art class, and most certainly knew nothing of sewing or quilt making, actually doing it.

Part three: Betting on Tomorrow

Over the weekend Chaco went back to Torreon and explained the project to his auntie. She gave him an old shirt that had belonged to Grandfather, and a Bluebird flour sack with the suggestion that they could make a quilt block from the picture.

Cowboy spent the entire day Saturday trying to sketch the horses in the barn and pasture behind their trailer. His father laughed at him, but at the dinner table agreed, "Those drawings do sorta look like horses."

Streak spent most of his time with Carlota. She offered to help with the stitching and showed him how to hold the cloth to cut it.

Rico, Juarez and Streak decided to take a walk down by the shelter, just to see what kind of hopeless losers might be there. Juarez waved to an older man with one arm. They spoke briefly. Then he turned to his friends, "He's a vet, name's Carlos Sanchez. Lost an arm in Nam, he says. Lost his family. No work. No jobs."

Rico leaned against the wall, "Damn. It's cold down here. Ask him what he'd think of a warm quilt." Then before Juarez could speak, Rico leaned closer and, using what little Spanish he could muster began to ask the question himself.

But Carlos interrupted, "Lots of folks down here could use something warm to wrap up in." He turned and pointed toward the door to the community soup kitchen. "We ain't just a bunch of druggies and winos. Look." He pointed with his finger toward a woman and three children huddled together against the wall. "Economy's bad, hits everyone, families and kids, old timers and vets like me." He paused to wipe a tear from his eye. "If ya got a quilt, give it to her and the kids. We gotta take care of the women and the kids. That's what real men do."

The three youths walked on, but the swagger was gone. Each was thinking of his own family, how close to homeless they were. Rico finally spoke, "Ya know, Momma's only one paycheck away from us being down here." Then he was silent again.

Juarez broke the silence, "Hey. We gotta make that quilt for them, for that lady and the kids."

By the time Monday arrived, each one of the 'Magnificent Seven' had decided that they wanted to be a part of this 'quilt thing.' It was during the last class that their names were read over the loudspeaker, a call to the office that made all the fellow students giggle, laugh and tease.

Ms. Albright was standing beside the door to her office with a rather stern looking man, tall, lean and without a sparkle in his eyes. With his long nose and hands clasped behind his back he looked like a sandhill crane. Chaco tried but couldn't restrain the smile. When he turned toward Dwight, they both started to laugh.

At this the crane man frowned even more and bobbed his head. "Delinquent barbarians. Ought to be behind bars, every last one of them." He bobbed his head again and added, "I won't stand for a stupid quilt as sufficient punishment for their vandalism." He raised his voice, clasped and re-clasped his hands behind his back as he spoke. To the boys this looked like a crane flapping its wings, trying to take flight. They could do nothing but laugh even harder.

The crane man, Harold Javis, was the president of the Carlton School Board, and an officer in the bank and owner of the Ford dealership. He scowled as he peered over his glasses. "I want these insults to America's youth locked up, where they won't do any more harm."

It was Dwight who spoke up, "It was the judge what said we had to make the quilt." He swallowed hard, then continued, "That's his decision, and we got to do what he says, whether we like it or not. . . . And so do you. It's the law, and we're a nation of laws. I learned that in government class. Didn't you?"

Rico jumped into the conversation with both feet. "Have you ever been down to the shelter? Do you know anything about the families, women and children that's got no home to go home to? We're makin' a quilt for a family. That's more than any of the kids in your school are doing."

Harold hurrummphed and shifted his acidic gaze toward Ms. Albright, who was smiling with obvious pride at what was now known all over the school as the Magnificent Seven.

"Perhaps we could issue a challenge to your students to see which high school could make the most quilts." She was taking a chance here, but her confidence in the kids knew no bounds at this point. "I'll bet you the seven thousand dollars in art supplies that . . ." but she was interrupted before she could finish.

"NOOOOOOO!" Nadine shouted as she approached the group standing in the hall outside the office. Poor Nadine was shaking at the very thought of putting her art supplies in jeopardy. Then she looked into the eyes of the boys standing before her. They were all smiling.

Harold cleared his throat again and bobbed his head once more. "I don't wager, gambling is for ignorant SOB's that don't have money to spare to begin with."

Chaco laughed, "Yeah, sorta like investing in the stock market, huh."

"Damn right!" Cowboy added. "But Ms. Albright here, she's bettin' on a sure thing."

Harold was cornered now. He looked for a way out, but there was none. Finally he leaned over and whispered to the principal, "Has to be brand new quilts. We have to let the entire student body participate . . ."

While he paused to consider more conditions that would favor Carlton High, Nadine added one of her own, "They have to be handmade, nothing bought from Walmart, or Goodwill either."

"Yeah, and no paying the hired help either. Just the kids."

Harold knew that Carlton High had at least 80 more students than Juniper Crossing High. This could be an easy victory. He agreed. Then beat a hasty retreat. But Nadine was already plotting ways to get the entire student body involved in the quilt project. Chaco opened the door to Ms. Albright's office. "We need to talk," he said.

Juarez described their meeting with the Viet Nam vet down at the shelter, and seeing the family that needed their quilt. Rico had tears in his eyes as he described some of the other people they saw in the shelter dining room. Then he looked at the rest of the Magnificent Seven. "Just want to let ya all know, we're gonna go down there Saturday and work in the shelter kitchen. We need to get to know these folks."

Streak started to laugh, but then became very quiet. He looked at his feet, "Bet there ain't enough room in that ratty old shelter for everyone without a home to go home to. Let's get the word out to everyone at JCHS. We're gonna need a lot of quilt stuff."

Before Saturday arrived, the entire student body was mobilized. In fact, they were CHARGED! A bake sale and a yard sale were organized to raise money for the supplies they would need. A most unlikely society of quilters had formed without prompting from the faculty. The bake sale money was used to purchase the batting. People from the neighborhood, parents, and students brought sheets from their own beds to serve as the backing for these quilts.

The yard sale had turned into a drive for colorful material for the quilt tops. The students in each class decided on themes that spoke of their interests and background. Scenes from New Mexico, characters from favorite cartoons, horses, eagles, cars and Christmas were themes. Others chose to simply create a crazy quilt by sewing pieces randomly to form a spontaneous blend of colors and textures.

Cowboy showed Nadine his horse sketches and asked how he could make them into a quilt. She showed him how to cut blocks from different pastel and earth tone colors, then use fabric markers to draw the horses and rodeo scenes.

Juarez sorted through the donated shirts, skirts, material and assorted fabrics to find patterns and images for his Arbol de Vida (tree of life) quilt.

Dwight decided to make a quilt for a child he had seen at the shelter. Each square would have a carefully appliqued Christmas ornament on it. His mother came to school to show everyone how to make the fine stitches that were almost invisible. She was so proud of her son for thinking of the homeless families. She was also proud of all the other students at Juniper Crossing High School.

Rico was still filled with anger as he sat and stitched the bright colored pieces together. Splashes of blood red and gothic black dominated his quilt. His stitches were uneven and often awkward. Nadine thought that his anger was about being forced to make a quilt. She sat down beside him and helped him hold the pieces while he plied the needle.

He looked into her eyes for a long silent moment before speaking. Finally he pushed the quilt from his knees and onto to the floor. "It ain't right!" he said.

The art teacher reached out and touched his shoulder. "I know this is difficult. I can understand that you don't feel comfortable doing this. But don't you think the judge was trying to make a point?" She paused, searching for the right words to bring him some comfort.

"NO!" he stared into her eyes. "You don't understand. These ninos, these little kids, they ain't got a home. I thought I didn't have nothing, yet look at them. Why don't somebody do something?" This was the anger she had known in another era when she was one of the young people, filled with idealism, trying to right all the wrongs of the world. This was the stuff of an activist, an angry dreamer. She took his hand in hers and looked into his eyes, into his troubled soul. She smiled and said, "You are. You're doing something." Her respect for this Magnificent Seven was growing. She added, before he had a chance to put the words of a response together, "None of us can save the world alone, but if each of us does just a little bit, wonderful things can happen."

"Yeah, but Santa ain't gonna visit those folks," he was remembering Christmases when Santa lost his way to their house. "Can't we do more than make these damn quilts?"

Nadine also remembered the lean holidays of her childhood. She shared his anger. His wish to do more was rekindling something in her heart that had been misplaced for too many years. Without a clue as to how, she stood, put her hands on his shoulders, stared into his eyes. "Yes we can!" she said. The rest of the day was spent pondering just what more they could do.

It was Chaco who accidently offered the solution that she was seeking. He was sitting in the art room, his quilt on the table where he had abandoned it in frustration. He was over by the window, working on a silver bracelet, using the artistic skill learned from his grandfather. He turned when she came into the room. "Sorry Ma'am," he said with his head down, "I ain't no good at that sewin' stuff. Had to get away from it for a while and do something I'm good at." He held the bracelet up for her to see. Finely sculpted flowers and intricate designs had been hammered and filed into the bare metal.

Every one of the students at Juniper Crossing High School had a special talent. Some had discovered what theirs was, other were still on a quest to find the artist within.

Cowboy entered the art room, saw them sitting by the window and started to back out. Nadine motioned for him to join them. She repeated her conversation with Rico and then showed him the bracelet Chaco was working on. There was a pause while Cowboy struggled to understand what she was talking about. What was it she wanted him to do now?

Finally she laughed out loud. "Do you guys have any idea what a gift you are to this old teacher?"

"Huh?" was all Cowboy could muster.

Before she could continue, Ms. Albright came into the room. Nadine briefly repeated the story. "See this," she said taking the bracelet from Chaco's hand again.

Before the end of the school day, the Magnificent Seven had spent over forty minutes in the office discussing Rico's concerns and trying to determine what could be done to "Guide Santa to the homeless shelter."

Ms. Albright leaned back in her chair as each of the boys took their turn offering solutions. Cowboy was going to offer pony rides beside the Santa tree at the shopping plaza, and on Christmas day would take his ponies to the shelter for the kids there to ride.

Tan was going to give Akido lessons to everyone in the shelter who wanted to learn.

Juarez was going to tell the Christmas stories to everyone in Spanish, and have everyone at the shelter help decorate a tree.

Dwight wanted to cook a Christmas dinner for everyone there.

Rico offered to do sketches of everyone at the shelter.

She was holding Chaco's bracelet in her hands. "What if we put this on eBay?" It was agreed that the money from selling Chaco's silver work could be used to buy toys for the kids.

That left Streak. He looked so sad as each of the others came forward with their talent. He had nothing to give.

Juarez patted his friend on the back, "Don't you remember what Ms. Albright said?"

Streak's shoulders slumped even more as he simply nodded his head. He mumbled, "Yeah."

She said, "It is in the giving that we discover the gift that we are." He paused, trying to find something more to say, something that would make everyone else understand that he was nothing. Finally, in an angry outburst he almost shouted, "But I ain't got nothin' ta give. I ain't nothin."

Part four: Friends

He turned and walked to the door. Then the mental image of the vet in the wheelchair came into his head. He turned and faced his friends. The words came as the idea formed in his mind. "What if we started a walking club for the folks down at the shelter? Even the guy in the wheelchair. I could kinda help him along the way. What do ya think?"

At first no one understood what he was talking about. Rico and Tan almost laughed at the idea. Then realized he wasn't joking. Finally Nadine spoke up, "What do you mean?" she asked, pausing briefly, "How would it work?"

Streak was standing tall again. There was a determination in his eyes that said he had discovered his gift within. "We, ahhh, I can get those folks to walk with me every morning before school starts. Each day we can take a walk down a different street, pick up trash along the way. We can take note of stuff that needs done. Those folks have all got skills and talents . . . ." He paused as he looked from face to face, "Just because they ain't got a home don't mean they ain't a gift. Like us, they maybe just ain't discovered what their gifts is yet."

"Walking's good for the head as well as exercise for the body. When I was in JD we took a walk around the exercise field every morning. It helped to get us ready for classes and we didn't fight as much." Rico was trying to encourage his friend.

"Man, this is New Mexico, like everyone out here's an artist of some sort," Tan added. "What if we worked with them folks to paint some of the buildings and . . . ."

The laughter from everyone else in the room stopped him in mid-sentence.

"Yeah. Nice going, Rico. That's what got us in trouble in the first place. Being an artist got us into this mess. Remember?" Dwight teased his friend.

Streak wasn't backing down. "I want to have a parade every morning. I want everyone who's on their way to work to see that these are our friends and neighbors. Just because they are poor and ain't got a home, don't mean they ain't still people."

Ms. Albright smiled broadly with the realization that her gang of troublemakers, her vandals, her Magnificent Seven, were, in their own way, becoming activists. These boys were rising from the ashes with the confidence to speak out. They had lived the problems, now they were putting mind and body into being the solution. It was working because the ideas were coming from them, not being forced onto them. They now owned the problem, but they also knew they WERE the solution.

Juniper Crossing High was now holding almost daily after school quilting bees. Parents, grandparents, aunts and even a couple of uncles were dropping by to give advice, offer materials, or share an idea.

Saturday saw another bake sale. This time it was to raise enough money to buy all the groceries necessary to make Thanksgiving dinner for the sixty-three men, women and children who called the downtown shelter home. Several of the girls in the remedial English class decided to collect children's books and take them to the shelter where they could read to the kids there. Some of the other students started a town wide drive for slightly used coats and sweaters for these "homeless, not friendless folks." The kids started dropping by the shelter after school and on the weekends, just to visit, just to get to know their new friends.

They would sit and chat, sometimes translating back and forth between the English and Spanish. Chaco found that his limited knowledge of traditional Navajo, the only way he could communicate with his uncles and grandmother, was a valuable gift for the three elderly Navajo who found themselves at the shelter most nights. He would listen to their stories and was able to find a grandson in a nearby town who welcomed one of the old men into his home.

All seven of the boys visited the shelter early Saturday morning. They were greeted by the aging Viet Nam vet Carlos Sanchez, the vet they met on their first visit to the shelter. He introduced them to a friend of his. Ben Harland was in a wheelchair. His two legs had been shattered when an IED exploded under his vehicle in Iraq. Now those legs were only a nightmare that visited him almost every night. Finding his way down a street too often brought an attack of memories. Horrible images, sounds of gunfire and screams of pain and death invaded his head and attacked his mind. Terror would grip his stomach and steal his breath. During such attacks from the past, every person who came near could be the enemy, might be armed and dangerous. Sometimes he would cry out in anger, sometimes in fear; but there was no escape.

"He's a friend of mine. Got lost in the shuffle at the VA hospital couple years ago. They didn't take PTSD seriously then." Carlos struggled with his one arm to maneuver the wheelchair out of the cold wind. Then he continued, "The only medication he's been able to find is in the bottle he guards with what's left of his life. He used to have a family, a home, and a garden where he raised enough food for the neighbors. No way he can garden now."

"Yes there is," Tan answered. "In my biology classroom they got a catalog that shows a little garden on wheels." By Monday afternoon Tan had found out all about this garden from the biology teacher and was in Ms. Albright's office trying to find the money to buy one for Ben. After the second phone call, she had a donation from the local lumber yard. It was ordered before she left the school that afternoon.

What had started out as a simple project with seven juvenile offenders tagging a rival school had become a massive project involving the entire school and much of the community. Ms. Albright was so proud of her kids. "At risk indeed!" she said as she spoke with the judge on the phone, "These boys really are my Magnificent Seven." She went on to share the activities of each of them. But there is still more to the story.

Fast forward to the week before Christmas. It had been cold, bitter cold. The coat drive had brought in donations of over a hundred coats, jackets and even a hand sewn parka from Alaska. Since there were only about sixty people using the shelter, these folks decided to send the rest of the warm winter wear to the shelter in the neighboring town.

Mrs. Evan's cooking class had started visiting the kitchen at the shelter. Students worked with the residents to prepare meals. Information about nutrition was shared along with stories from many cultures. It was during one of the cleanups after dinner that one of the older ladies staying at the shelter told a story of how they would gather some of the wild plants for their dinner. One of the Navajo men described how they would "fish for prairie dogs" and cook them for dinner. Soon delightful, delicious and even a few less than appetizing food stories were being swapped back and forth.

It was Juarez who made the suggestion that these might make interesting meals that could be shared, the students with their new friends. Elvira, one of the homeless visitors suggested that the entire community of Juniper Crossing could be invited to the shelter for dinner and a multilingual Christmas party with lots of good music and a potluck feast like you could find only in New Mexico.

Part five: It's a Feast

"What a crazy idea." Greg at the *Juniper Crossing Messenger* said when the boys visited the newspaper office. "What an absolutely absurd idea," he repeated to himself, looking over his bifocals at this rather scruffy collection of youth gone bad.

Dwight and Chaco both started to speak at the same time, but Greg interrupted, "Whose idea is this?" But before they got the words together for a response he continued, "You want to hold a community wide Christmas feast at that old run down homeless shelter on Christmas Eve?" He leaned back in his chair, smiled, then added, "Hell of a good idea."

He wished he had a photographer to get some pictures for a front page article, but right now there was no one available. Then Rico told them about the old lady staying at the shelter who had a digital camera and took a lot of photos that had been printed out and were now framed and hanging on the walls. Greg decided to ask her to shoot the photos. He even offered to pay her for them.

The article that appeared in the paper the Saturday before Christmas was an invitation, along with interviews some of the students had conducted with residents and visitors to the shelter. There was a special request from Elvira that everyone prepare something from their "traditional dinner table so that we can all get to know each other by the food we eat."

The last paragraph was about the quilt that started it all. Greg headlined the article *"Betting on the Quilt."*

The last week before what was now referred to everywhere as simply "The Feast" was a frenzy of activity. Quilting was being done at a feverish pace. Some teams of students were completing their third and fourth quilts, while all of the Magnificent Seven had finished theirs except Chaco. True, he had sold three pieces of silver work on eBay and brought in almost $300.00. It was Streak who offered to sit with his friend and help with the less than half done quilt. Soon Juarez and Rico joined him. Cowboy and Dwight entered the art room and without a word took up needle and scissors.

Tan was the last to join the group. He had been busy delivering the Green Thumb Garden, some soil and seeds to Ben Harland. Together they adjusted the height so that Ben's wheelchair rolled easily underneath the garden itself. They rolled it over to the large window in the dining room. Tan and Ben together filled it with soil, then Ben selected the seeds he wanted to plant; lettuce, cilantro, carrots, onions and chard. Tan was pleased to see Ben smiling, feeling safe in his garden, with images of the plants that would soon be growing and the memories of gardens past.

By the time the school was being locked up for the Christmas break, the boys were almost finished with Chaco's quilt. Nadine stood in the doorway silently watching. She was so proud of all that they had done, and all that they could now do because they had discovered themselves.

113

The homeless living at the shelter and the frequent visitors started spreading plastic tablecloths and setting the tables, along with the students from Juniper Crossing High who had arrived with two pickup loads of quilts.

The Celebration at the shelter was to begin at 1:00 P.M., but the students and the folks at the shelter were afraid no one would show up. They began preparing excuses.

Everyone would be busy the day before Christmas. It was too cold and it was snowing.

The roads might become treacherous.

But the real reason they were afraid no one would come was because of the truth no one was willing to voice. These folks were homeless, assumed winos and druggies, lazy or failures at life. Their clothing was ragged and often in need of the laundry. Many of the people were also in need of a shower, or at least a haircut. They were the unknown, faceless un-residents of the community.   One of the men entered the dining room, pulled a chair into the corner and began strumming on an old guitar while the others were setting the tables. Juarez joined this old man and began singing along in Spanish. His gave voice to the carol as the guitar gave it life. Soon many of those setting the tables were singing along as well.

The people started arriving at about 10:30 a.m. with everything from Christmas trees and ornaments to poinsettias and Christmas cactus, and just because this is New Mexico, chile ristras were in abundance. Kori brought a beautiful chile plant she had grown in her kitchen window. It was hanging full of bright red chiles.

The first surprise was when the kitchen door opened and the students and homeless friends carried trays of Gingerbread people, biscochitos and sugar cookies to each table. Every cookie was fresh baked and decorated with hope.

The room filled with a delightful assortment of people, all ages, speaking several languages, wearing a wide range of clothes, each bringing a gift, and in so many ways, each being a gift. The Judge entered wearing a flannel shirt, blue jeans and a chef's hat. He was carrying a tray of bar-b-qued ribs and his granddaughter was by his side with a huge bowl of red and green biscuits. Greg watched as the lady with the little digital camera was circulating around the room getting shots that would record this special event forever. He held the brightly wrapped box in his hand, a special gift for his new photographer.

By noon the room was overflowing with people. Music was disorganized and far from studio quality, but since everyone was singing, playing or attempting to dance, it didn't matter. For these folks music was a participation sport, and so was life.

The coffee, hot chocolate, soft drinks and fruit juices flowed along with a delightful assortment of cookies, popcorn and special foods from every corner of the globe. It was almost 1:00 p.m. when the judge came to the front of the room and pounded his gavel on the table. Rico shouted, "Order in the court." And everyone laughed. Then the entire dining room became very quiet. A quilt was folded on the table before him. He motioned for the boys to come forward and started to speak, but Chaco patted him on the arm and said, "Please, man, a . . . your honor . . . sir, no speeches today. OK?"

114

The doors swung open with a BANG! Harold Javis, from the Carlton High School Board entered the room followed by a parade of students, each carrying a stack of quilts. They lined the back wall while Harold started walking toward the front table, but Ms. Albright motioned for him to wait.

Ms. Albright joined the judge at the table and motioned for the boys to hold up the quilt on the table. "Six weeks ago these boys got into a little bit of trouble, but today they have redeemed themselves." She introduced her Magnificent Seven as they unfurled the huge quilt for all to see. "This is Chaco's quilt. He said that he couldn't make a quilt, so his friends helped him out. Together they accomplished what he couldn't do alone. Their new friends down here at the shelter gave them a gift that they want to repay. You gave them HOPE when some of them didn't even know the meaning of the word."

The quilt, made with left over squares, multicolored patches and odd sized pieces all fit together somehow. As it was held up for all to see, the message was plain. In huge solid colored letters, made up of assorted pieces of all kinds of fabric was the word H-O-P-E.

Chaco read from the piece of paper he took from the back pocket of his jeans. "Hope is a thing of great beauty, a delightful array of colors and shapes and textures. Together we are all the hope of tomorrow, and the hope for each other." He was shy and he stumbled through the words, but as he added, "My girl, Carlota, she wrote this. I think it's a poem," everyone in the dining room applauded.

The man with the guitar began strumming an unfamiliar tune. Then he added the words to a song he wrote, *"Hope is a Quilt Made with Many Hands."* The second time through everyone was singing along. After all, it was their song.

There had been an arrogant sneer on Harold Javis's face when he entered. Now he worked his way through the crowd to the front of the dining room.

He raised his hand and pointed to the judge. "I believe we have a bet, your honor. How many quilts did they make?" Then he looked into the faces of the Magnificent Seven, and the faces of the homeless, and the faces of the people from Juniper Crossing. His gaze went from the quilt to the people. A strange thing happened. He could see the word HOPE spelled out on the diverse faces of all these people. A great truth struck him speechless. "My God," he whispered to himself, "These people, all these people, they're a quilt too.

It was Ms. Albright who spoke up. "Our students worked hard, spending their weekends and after school hours to make 86 quilts."

The judge wrote down the number on a piece of paper and waited for Harold to respond.

He cleared his throat, then with a puzzled look on his face, motioned for his students to come forward. "Carlton High's students worked long and hard too, and they . . ." he paused and looked over the people in the room again. Again he saw the word HOPE spelled out in their faces. Yes, this too was a quilt. Finally he continued. "My students created 86 quilts, but I think you miscounted the number of quilts JC High made."

The judge spoke, "I think we have to have an official recount. Ms. Albright, you and your boys will count your quilts against the left side of the room. Mr. Javis, if you will count against the right wall we will appoint monitors.

"That won't be necessary," Harold said as he looked at the people again. "This room is the 87th quilt created by JC High. Just look at the faces of your community. There is hope written on these faces. This is a dynamic, living quilt of humanity here. I think that Juniper Crossing has won the bet, but I think that everyone here has won, too. Merry Christmas." Then he turned to Ms. Albright, winked, and added, "Make good use of those art supplies."

The delightful diversity of humanity is nowhere more evident than in New Mexico. This state, or perhaps it's a state of mind, is truly a patchwork quilt, pieced together with many hands, singing many songs, seeking the warmth of peace on a dark winter's night in prayers spoken in many languages. We are each just a scrap of cloth, but together we are a work of art. This is the season of the year when we give ourselves permission to join with our neighbors to celebrate the beauty of peace.

The Gift of Angels

Too often we fail to understand the gifts we are given. In a small town east of the mountains in New Mexico, in a school for disabled children, underfunded and under staffed, a little girl grasped a profound truth, even if she couldn't count, or remember her colors. Hopefully you will enjoy this little story. Perhaps it will bring the gift of a smile to you. If so, please pass it on.

"Angels," he said with a touch of sadness in his voice. "Don't believe in such things."

Lucinda looked into Mr. Haffey's eyes. Her brow was furrowed as she struggled to understand how this old man could say such a thing. Finally she blurted out, "They're real. I've seen 'em."

He laughed out loud, "Sure, on the top of a Christmas tree."

"No," Lucinda spoke slowly, trying to find the words to explain what she had seen. "I saw him first the night my Mamma almost died in the car crash." She paused, waiting to see how this old man would respond. "He is my special angel, and he protects me."

She spoke with such innocence and conviction that Mr. Haffey felt sorry for her and regretted his thoughtless comment. He had lived a life of loneliness and poverty that had overwhelmed all hope, but he didn't want to deny this young girl her mythical creature. After all, a chubby ten year old with Down's Syndrome and leg braces needs all the help she can get. In his mind, he limped down the hall pushing the mop bucket in front of him. At the age of sixty-eight, this unhappy old man had little to be thankful for the week before Christmas. True, he had a job, "custodian" they called him. There he was at the end of a useless life, janitor for the El Mesquite School for Exceptional Children. At least the children called him Mr. Haffey, or at least those who could speak. It was good to have a little respect. It helped ease the pain in his arthritic joints, but it didn't help the loneliness that haunted his every step.

He was reluctant to admit it, but he liked his job in this school. It wasn't demanding work. He also enjoyed watching the children at play, hearing them sing their songs of childhood. Even with the problems and disabilities these special children carried with them each and every day, they were able to smile. Some, like Lucinda, were what he called retarded, others possessed minds that refused to cooperate with their bodies, some couldn't speak, while others were unable to grasp a pencil or name the colors of the ornaments they made for their Christmas tree. He was the one responsible for cleaning up when one of them vomited or spilled the water they gave the plants growing on their windowsill garden.

Keeping them safe during the day and waving to them as they left for home each afternoon made him feel that maybe he had a purpose after all. That helped his depression, his sense of failure at a career as a musician. Guilt for living while friends had died in his arms in a distant war haunted his sleep. For years he had surrendered to the bottle, to homeless wandering, to the special solitude that can be found only in the city. Now at least, in old age, he had climbed out of the bottle, had the responsibility of a job and a warm place to stay at night. But, this didn't bring with it the freedom from his past, nor did this bring happiness.

It was a long and lonely walk home to his basement room, a generous gift of shelter from the realtor. Well, not really a gift, rather a trade. He got to be maintenance man for the two aging apartment buildings that many considered the eyesore of this small community's downtown. In exchange he got to live in a basement studio apartment in one of them.

Images of yesterdays, wasted and lost, washed over his mind as he stood there gazing out the big window at the end of the hall. His mind ambled into other times and places, but Lucinda didn't mind. She was patient as is the way of so many with developmental disabilities. She understood that sometimes the mind will wander off, all on its own, but she knew it will always find its way back. Sometimes her mind was off on one of these journeys.

She took a piece of paper out of her backpack and handed it to him, "This is for you," she said with a broad smile. "I drew this myself." It was a flower, crudely drawn in bright colors. It was held in two hands with a big red smile above. No face or hair, no eyes, only the smile; this little girl's perception of what was important.

"Thank you," Mr. Haffey spoke, overwhelmed by the gift. Tears formed in the corners of his eyes. One dropped onto the drawing he held in his hands. He couldn't remember the last time someone had given him a gift. He didn't know quite how to accept it, even one as insignificant as this one.

Her ride pulled up to the curb. She smiled, waved and was gone. He folded the paper and put it in his pocket, but he was now wearing the hint of a smile as he mopped the empty hallway. "Angels indeed." He spoke to the emptiness within, but somehow, for at least a small moment in time, he no longer felt the crushing weight of loneliness.

Lucinda sat in the back seat talking with what her mother called her imaginary friend. What she was really doing was telling her angel friend all about Mr. Haffey and how he needed an angel of his own, even if he wasn't a kid anymore.

118

Afriel, her angel, sat holding the small flower, bright orange, with the pungent fragrance that proclaimed it a marigold. Finally Lucinda asked him if there was any way he could find an angel for her new friend. He handed her the flower, smiled and whispered, "I'll see what I can do, but no promises." Then without another word, he closed his eyes and took a nap.

When Mother unbuckled the seatbelt and helped her out of the car, Lucinda handed her the single orange marigold.

"Where did you get this?" She knew it was far beyond the season for this rugged annual and was quite surprised to see one. Then she guessed that it must be from the garden that Lucinda and her friends tended in the classroom.

"My angel gave it to me," she responded as she placed her little hand in Mommy's and they slowly walked up the driveway.

Her mother laughed, "And what does your angel look like?"

"Oh he's just a little bigger than me, but I don't think he has braces. Oh, he does have a great big smile. The biggest smile in the whole world." She giggled and squeezed her mommy's hand.

"I thought all angels were girls," Her mother responded as she opened the door. "Does your angel have great big wings?"

Lucinda thought long before she answered. Sometimes it was difficult for her to find just the right words. "There are girl and boy angels. Just like kids. And, they don't really have wings." After a brief pause with her head turned toward her imaginary friend, she laughed her most delightful laugh. "He says if angels had wings they couldn't get into their tee shirts and jackets."

Her Mother laughed with her, then smiled down at her little girl. "If that's what he told you then it must be true." She enjoyed these little journeys of imagination that her daughter took. They gave her the hope that she needed to cling to, the hope that her daughter would somehow wake up some morning and be normal.

After dinner that evening, Lucinda told her father about poor Mr. Haffey and how lonely he was. Then she added, "He doesn't have any friends, not even an angel to talk to."

"And do you have an angel friend?" he asked.

She giggled, "Of course. His name is Afriel. He told me he is a special angel. His job is to bring hope to children."

Her father smiled and went into the kitchen to help wash the dishes.

Lucinda continued to sit on the sofa engaged in conversation with her imaginary friend, or at least a friend who was invisible to her parents. Her mother aimed the camera at her daughter and took several photos. Later that evening, just before Lucinda went to bed, they printed them out on the computer.

"Can I have one of those photos you made?" Lucinda asked as she was tucked in for the night. She then turned to her invisible friend, her special angel Afriel, and whispered, "I have an idea." Then she was asleep.

Part two: Gifts

Lucinda liked her school because when it was warm, she got to help plant and tend the flowers along the sidewalk. They even grew some vegetables last spring. In the winter, their gardening moved inside and she helped her classmates grow "flower friends" in their windowsill garden. However, today she was anxious for Mr. Haffey to arrive because she had another gift for him. While he was hanging his coat in the closet, she came up to him with the photograph of herself sitting on the sofa. Beside her picture she had used her crayons to draw a huge smile. "This is for you."

Mr. Haffey took the photo in his hands with a look of embarrassment on his face. "Thank you." He lowered his head, unable to look her in the eyes, "But I have no gift for you."

"OH, you're my friend," she was trying really hard to find the right words, "YOU are the gift." She was trying to find the thought she had just a moment ago. It was something she wanted to say, but she had lost the words somewhere between her mind and her mouth, so she just smiled that big, beautiful smile of hers.

A cold rain started just before lunch period. When it was time for Lucinda and her classmates to water the garden and pot up the Christmas cactus they had been growing to make gifts, one of the other children shouted, "Look! It's snowing." The dark dismal rain and mist had turned into snowflakes, big, heavy flakes that silently descended on the now frozen ice that covered the sidewalk and parking lot.

While Mrs. Gutierrez carried the trays of plants from the windowsill over to the work tables, the children were busy putting bright colored Christmas stickers on the green and red plastic pots. Next they filled each one of these pots with soil, getting some on the table, a little bit on their aprons and more on the floor.

They had started Christmas cactus cuttings soon after school began in August. The teacher had brought three big plants into the classroom along with pictures of red, pink and white Christmas cactus flowers, and they each took a cutting of all three colors. They worked together to fill their trays with sandy soil and helped each other plant the little Y-shaped sprigs of cactus. Lucinda couldn't remember the name of the color green, but she enjoyed the feeling of life in each of these soon-to-be plants. When she watered her baby Christmas cactus, she would gently touch each one of the cuttings. In her mind she could already see each one with a beautiful flower on it. Sometimes she would talk to her little plants as they grew.

Garran was blind and couldn't walk, but Lucinda helped him to the garden on the windowsill and put his hand on the plants. He would smile as his fingers tenderly followed the curves of the Christmas cactus pads and patted their thick fleshiness. Once he accidently pulled one out of the soil. Lucinda thought it was so cool to see the little roots. She helped Garran feel them. She told him he was seeing with his fingers and they both laughed. Then they replanted it.

Now most of the rooted cuttings had buds on them and some were even showing off their vivid colors. They were ready to be transplanted into the pots the children had been decorating. Snow was now falling so fast that they couldn't even see the junipers beyond the playground. Afriel, her angel was there to help her. He was looking over her shoulder while she was waiting her turn.

She turned to see what he was watching and saw Mr. Haffey shoveling snow from the ice covered sidewalk. Just as she was getting ready to carefully use the plastic fork to remove her plants from the garden, she saw him begin to fall on the ice.

She screamed, "Afriel, catch him!"

In an instant, before the old man hit the ice, it was like something had caught him. For less than a moment it was as though he was being held in mid-air, then he slowly straightened up. She saw him turn and look behind him. She could see Afriel, or at least, she could see that big broad smile beside Mr.Haffey.

Now she returned her attention to retrieving her Christmas cactus plants and began humming as she transplanted them into the bright green pot she had decorated. Next the children put shiny stones around their plants. Then they each picked out a silk flower from the tray the teacher, Mrs. Gutierrez, placed on the table. Most picked bright red poinsettias, but Lucinda looked at each one, held different flowers in her hand and finally chose the smallest of the silk flowers Mrs. Gutierrez had brought. It was the only orange flower on the tray. The leaves were missing and the petals were frayed, but she recognized this as the flower Afriel had given her.

Lucinda looked out the window again and saw Mr. Haffey scattering the sawdust on the ice so that none of the children would slip. He used sawdust rather than salt because it wouldn't hurt the plants that he had helped the children plant along the walk and around the playground. He looked so lonely, out there in the snow all by himself.

She helped Garran place his plants in the pot. Then she looked back at the now empty tray sitting on the windowsill. But it wasn't quite empty. There were still several cuttings left. Each had a bud, but each now looking as lonely as Mr. Haffey.

"Mrs. Gutierrez," Lucinda spoke as she tugged on the teacher's sleeve, "what will happen to these plants?" She was pointing toward the remaining plants.

"Do you want them?" the teacher responded with a smile.

"OH YES!" Lucinda squealed with joy as she gave her teacher a big hug. "Thank you."

She quickly put stickers on another shiny green plastic pot. Then she took a red crayon and drew a big red smile on it.

She clutched a beautifully decorated plant in each hand as she walked out the door to wait on the sidewalk for Mommy. Mr. Haffey was humming a Christmas song as he continued to shovel snow and make the walkways safe for the children and easy for the wheelchairs. He saw her coming and started toward her to thank her again for the photo.

She handed him one of the Christmas cactus she held in her hands. "For you," she said with a smile that matched the one on the pot. "It's a Flower Friend, just for you." Then she saw Mommy's car and turned to get in.

"Merry Christmas," he said with a wave and a smile that also matched the one on the pot.

Part three: Making Angel Cookies

After the dinner dishes were cleared from the table, it was decided that they would bake cookies for the Christmas party at school the next day, the last school day before the big holiday. Lucinda's mother took the big cookbook, the one with the bright color pictures in it, down from the shelf. While they were looking at all the different kinds of cookies they could make, Lucinda told them about how Afriel helped Mr. Haffey when he was falling on the ice. Her parents smiled at each other, pleased with their little girl's imagination.

Her father slowly went from page to page in the cookbook. Finally Lucinda turned to her side, whispering with her angel friend. Then she clapped her hands and shouted, "That's the one. That's the cookies we must make." The picture showed a platter of juniper glazed gingerbread cookies in the shape of angels, complete with wings.

"I want to give everyone an angel for Christmas, specially Mr. Haffey, 'cause he's so lonely." With that she clapped her hands again. The decision was made. Now they were ready to start baking. She whispered to the occupant of the empty chair beside her, then giggled. "Afriel says they don't really have wings, but that's ok."

They gathered all the ingredients, and while the Christmas music played they began.

Lucinda's Gingerbread Angels recipe

Ingredients:
Cookies
2 1/4 cups unbleached or whole wheat flour
1 tsp ground ginger
1 tsp ground allspice
½ tsp ground cinnamon
½ tsp baking soda
½ cup unsalted butter at room temperature
½ cup unsweetened applesauce
½ cup brown sugar (light or dark)
Juniper glaze
3/4 cup non-fat half & half
1/3 cup crushed juniper berries, fresh or dried (they can be ground in a coffee mill)
1 lb powdered sugar

Putting it all together:
Preheat oven to 350F
lightly greased cookie sheet

Mix flour, spices and baking soda in a mixing bowl
In a separate large bowl blend butter, applesauce and sugar until fluffy
Combine with dry ingredients with above mixture
Divide dough into four pieces, wrap in waxed paper and chill for 2 to 3 hours
Roll dough to about 1/8 to 1/4 inch thickness
Use an angel shaped cookie cutter, or other shapes of your choice
Place on cookie sheet and bake until almost firm (approximately 12 to 15 minutes)

Glaze can be made up ahead of time so that it has time to cool
Bring juniper berries and half and half to a light simmer in a small sauce pan
Cover and chill for at least 1 hour
Place powdered sugar in a bowl and slowly add the liquid, whisking to keep it smooth
Continue adding liquid until the glaze is thick enough to spread
Use a table knife or small pastry brush to apply to the cookies
Decorate with your choice of raisins, colored sugar or other decorations of your choice. Be creative.

Note: The juniper glaze adds a delightful new dimension to the flavor of these traditional cookies. The use of applesauce and fat-free half & half reduces the fat content by over 50%.

While her parents measured and mixed all the ingredients, Lucinda sorted through the big wooden box of cookie cutters looking for one shaped like an angel. She had them spread all over the table. Finally, almost at the bottom of the box, she found it. Next they mixed and chilled the dough. While they shared some warm cider, the oven was preheated. Lucinda helped as they rolled the gingerbread cookie dough on the table. While Lucinda and her mother shaped, baked, cooled and stacked the cookies, her father was busy at the stove making the juniper glaze. He used the juniper berries that he and Lucinda had gathered in the fall to make hot juniper tea on the cold winter nights when it was snowing outside.

Soon they had dozens and dozens of gingerbread angels lined up on the table and the juniper glaze was cooling in the refrigerator. After the cookies had cooled and the glaze was ready, they began to decorate each one of the gingerbread angels. It was agreed that each angel would be different. They filled the table with glazed cookies, some sparkled with colored sugar crystals, some looked majestic with chocolate shavings, and others were outlined in glaze with raisin buttons. Lucinda was frowning as she looked over the finished gingerbread angels. She tugged on her mother's apron. "There's something missing," she said, so tired that she was having trouble finding the right words. She looked up with the biggest frown her parents had ever seen.

"What's missing, Honey?" her mother responded as she wiped a little flour from Lucinda's forehead.

"They aren't smiling," she answered. "My angel is always smiling."

The problem was easily solved as her father mixed some strawberry flavored icing and put a dash of red food coloring in it. It became Lucinda's job to paint a great big smile on each and every one of these gingerbread angels.

It was late before all the gingerbread angels were glazed and given their smiles, so late that Lucinda was now sound asleep with her head on the table and the pink icing in her hand.

Her father carried her up to bed while her mother arranged most of the cookies on the big platter, covered them and decided that it was time for them to go to bed as well. The dishes were all done, the cookie sheets put away and the Flower Friend was carefully placed on the kitchen windowsill.

Part four: The Christmas Party

Lucinda arrived at the school early. Her mother helped her carry the platter of gingerbread angels into their classroom. Mrs. Gutierrez was busy setting out the cups for juice and bright napkins on each of the group tables while her aides were busy hanging apples, oranges and bananas on the Christmas tree that had appeared overnight in front of the teacher's desk.

Just as Lucinda was being helped out of her coat, Mr. Haffey came into the room. He was wearing a Santa hat and he was carrying a big, funny shaped case, but there was something more. He was wearing a big smile, a very big smile, just like Afriel's smile.

Soon all the children were out of their coats and being helped to their places. Garran was feeling the cookies on his plate and smiled when he came to Lucinda's gingerbread angel. Each of these children was called disabled, some physically, others mentally, but each and every one of them was able to know wonderful moments of joy. They all had a profound love to share, hugs to give and the gift of a smile.

As these children enjoyed the cookies on their plates, drank their juice and ate the fruit they picked from the Christmas tree, they all wore smiles, just like Afriel, just like the gingerbread angels. There was so much happiness in the room that somehow it seemed brighter than usual. Even though outside it was dark and dismal with the threat of more rain and snow, light had most definitely been brought into this room on this day.

Mr. Haffey was now sitting on the corner of the teacher's desk looking out at the smiles these children so freely gave to each other, and to him. He reached down and undid the snaps that held the case closed, removed his scratched and battered old guitar and returned their smiles. He hadn't played this old guitar for over a decade, but it called to him this morning as he struggled to find some way to repay the kindness of a little girl named Lucinda and the angel she so willingly shared.

For a moment he was afraid to put his fingers to the strings. He started to shake and he felt like he was going to throw up. Then he looked out at these children, each with limitations, each one called handicapped and denied what we consider a normal life. He realized he wasn't alone after all. Their smiles were the smiles of angels. They were, each and every one of them, an angel. They would guide his fingers and he would sing once again. The fear left him as the courage that comes from friendship overwhelmed him. What began with his fingers and his solitary old voice soon became so much more.

Together they sang song after song. Some might question the use of that term "together" but it is most profoundly accurate. It wasn't studio produced artificial perfection with trained voices, or even a skilled guitarist. No, but it was the voices of a small multitude of angels sharing their joy. At some level, perhaps they knew that they were each other's angels. Perhaps they also knew, as Lucinda did, that the essence of an angel isn't the wings, but the smile.

May you be surrounded by the smiles of angels this Christmas. May you, like Lucinda, be the bringer of the light for a season of peace. Each of us has within us great gifts to give, and each day is the gift of opportunity for us to share a smile, and that's all it takes. Sing the songs and nibble on a smiling gingerbread angel. Remember, the wings are optional, but the smile is essential.

Lucinda is translated as "bringer of light."

A New Mexico Christmas Moment

A trip to the Post Office the week before Christmas can be a walk through a horrible nightmare. We approach with dread the long lines and surly attitudes from both the harried customers and the overworked and exhausted postal workers. Fortunately I deal with one of the greatest post offices in the whole country. The Cottonwood Post Office is a small station located in a strip mall. But walking through those doors yesterday (Dec. 20th) was a most refreshing experience.

The line was almost to the door, such a delightful diversity of ages, colors, sizes and shapes; each with packages to mail, questions to ask and other places to be. Kevin and Miguel were behind the counter making eye contact with each person, sharing a smile and a greeting, sometimes a joke. They had placed a basket filled with small candy canes on the counter, to sweeten attitudes, I'm certain, but what a beautiful and simple gesture.

There was a young girl, about 6 or 7 years of age, skipping from the basket of candy canes to the patrons in the line, serving as a volunteer good will ambassador for the Postal Service. She then straightened the envelopes and boxes in the Priority Mail display.

The last person to come in the door, struggling to balance three large boxes, said in a voice loud enough for all to hear, "Thank God, I was afraid I'd miss the party!" He paused to see the reaction, then added, "You know. The Post Office Christmas Party."

Just then someone's cell phone rang with *Jingle Bells* as the ringtone. The little girl began singing. Then several others did as well. The elderly lady in front of me turned and smiled, "I'm sending this to my grandson. He's in Scranton, PA. It's a blanket. I knitted myself. He's having a baby next week." The lady in front of her joked, "You mean his wife is having the baby don't you?" She then took a couple Sesame Street stickers from her purse and put them on the box the elderly lady was holding.

A shy fella was holding a stack of Christmas cards. He turned to the young lady next to him and asked, "Do I have to use Christmas stamps on these cards?" She told him he could use any stamps he wished, as long as they were the right size. They left their place in line to look at the stamps displayed on the wall. Soon they were talking about being students at UNM and being a long way from family for the holidays. I think they had a date planned before they got to the counter.

Along this steadily moving line, conversations were happening. Folks were enjoying the candy canes and the relaxed atmosphere as personal stories were shared and momentary friendships formed. This is the magic of the season, but it is also a compliment to the staff of this little post office, focusing on the patron at the counter as if he or she were a guest in their living room. The necessary questions were asked and the service rendered, not with impatience or irritation, but with simple acts of courtesy and friendship. In this season of the year, when we celebrate peace and good will, how beautiful to see peace personified by so many people who have been fortunate enough to be in the line at this post office.

Thank you Kevin, Miguel and the rest of you great folks who make the last minute visit to the post office truly a Post Office Christmas Party. What a gift to have angels behind the counter.

Peace

Each of us has a story to tell, and each of us is a story. The people of New Mexico know the value in sharing the stories that define us as a part of this marvelous creation. Wherever you are, whoever you are, child, adult or elder, you are a gift. You can be enchanted by the light, and you can be the light of love and the glow of peace that makes this such an enchanting season. Share your stories with others, and take the time to listen to their stories too.

Thank you for being the gift you are, and Merry Christmas.

Peace, Hank Bruce & Tomi Jill Folk

other books written by Hank Bruce

Peace Beyond All Fear, a Tribute to John Denver's Vision

Oblivion, a Novel Place to Live

Gardens for the Senses, Gardening as Therapy

Courage to Create

books written by Hank Bruce & Tomi Jill Folk

Global Gardening

The Family Caregiver's Journal: A Guide to Facing the Terminal Illness of a Loved One

Gardening Projects for Horticultural Therapy Programs

Garden Projects for the Classroom and Special Learning Programs

Windowsill Whimsy, Gardening & Horticultural Therapy Projects for Small Spaces

The Abundant Harvest Garden for The American Southwest

Seniors Illustrated, Volume 1

Seniors Illustrated Volume 2

The Miracle of the Moringa Tree

Along the Garden Path

Visits with the Old Indian Storyteller

Stasha Dog's Secret Dream, A Hot Air Balloon Adventure

Made in the USA
Charleston, SC
22 November 2011